"Hannah, you've got to hide!" whispered Alexis. I quickly checked around in a panic, but I couldn't see anyplace to go.

"The balcony!" hissed Maria. I could hear the coach's footsteps outside the door to the hall. I dove through the open door onto the balcony just as Coach Gretel called, "Bed check!" I gingerly slipped off to the side, out of sight. As I plastered myself against the wall, I heard a loud grunt. It sounded like it was right by my feet! I froze. *What was that?* I thought, totally terrified. I mean, here I was, at least thirty feet off the ground on this tiny balcony, in the dark, in a foreign country. And now, on top of it all, I was hearing strange grunts? Somehow, I had managed to get myself into *another* interesting situation, to say the least.

"Lights out, girls!" I heard Coach Gretel say. "Get a good sleep for practice tomorrow." She flipped off the bedroom light, so now it was even darker on the balcony.

"Who's there?" I whispered into the dark. I looked down and saw the shadow of a hand right next to my foot. Then another shadowy hand. Somebody was climbing up the rope—onto the balcony!

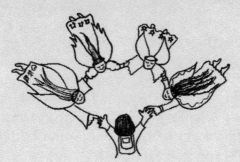

Hannah and the Angels
Missing Piece in Greece

by Linda Lowery Keep

Based on a concept by
Linda Lowery Keep
and Carole Newhouse

Random House New York

Cover art © 2000 by Peter Van Ryzin

Copyright © 2000 by Renegade Angel, Inc.,
and Newhouse/Haft Associates, Inc.
HANNAH AND THE ANGELS is a trademark of Random House, Inc.,
Renegade Angel, Inc., and Newhouse/Haft Associates, Inc.
RANDOM HOUSE and colophon are registered trademarks
of Random House, Inc.

www.randomhouse.com/kids

Library of Congress Catalog Card Number: 00-025572
ISBN: 0-375-80257-6

Printed in the United States of America
May 2000
10 9 8 7 6 5 4 3 2 1

For the children I taught in Athens:
May the angels help them
find their own music and dance
toward their dreams.

Contents

Hannah and the Angels

Missing Piece in Greece

Chapter 1

Sirens

"Strike three!"

I was at the Geneva Lake Festival, which *everybody* in town turns out for. I was playing my favorite event of the day—boys-against-girls kickball. But the boys were beating us pretty bad. Actually, they were totally stomping all over us. And I wasn't helping my team out much, either. In fact, I had just struck out.

There I was, face-down on the ground with a mouthful of grass and dirt. Somehow, the ball was right under me—it felt like a huge round bellyache. Then I tasted blood. Oh, great. Blood.

Everybody came rushing over to me, a little panicked.

"Are you okay, Hannah?" asked my teacher Ms. Crysler (aka Mrs. Crybaby).

"Keep still, honey," said my mom as she held

my head. She pulled the ball out from under me while my dad checked my mouth to see where the blood was coming from.

"No loose teeth," he announced.

All the girls on my team were looking down at me miserably. I guess they figured I was too injured to keep playing.

"Hey, no sweat, guys, I'm fine," I said as I pushed myself up to a sitting position. Even though I was in a little bit of pain, I was more embarrassed than I was hurt. I couldn't believe what a lame attempt at a kick I had just made! And in front of everyone from my town, too. What timing.

Smooth move!

"You bit your lip when you went down," my dad said. "But you'll be okay, sport." He handed me a handkerchief to dab at the blood with.

Ms. Montgomery, the referee, blew her whistle. "All right, everybody, back away!" she shouted. "Come on, let's get on with the game!"

I had just struck out, so my team was taking the field. As I headed toward the infield, Jimmy Fudge strutted his goofy self past me. "Have a nice trip, Martin?" he sneered.

I glared at him, giving him my stony face that I reserve for major dorks.

"It's just too bad you didn't take a few of your wimpy girl teammates with you...on your _trip_," he continued.

Now, I would have let Jimmy Fudge have it right there and then. But I don't do trash talk. Jimmy likes to think he's a master at getting under my skin with his dumb comments, but the truth is, he doesn't even come close. I mean, we're all just playing a fun game in the park, so why would I let a first-class doofus like the Fudge ruin my good time? But he thought he was so funny, yukking his way across the field, high-fiving his teammates. So I just let him think what he wanted to.

I noticed that David Chang didn't give Jimmy a high-five. Instead, he avoided the Fudge and looked over at me.

"You okay, Hannah?" he asked as we passed each other.

"Yeah, I'm fine. Thanks for asking," I said. "But you better watch out next time I'm up!" I warned.

David smiled. He's a really good sport. His twin sister, Katie (who also happens to be my best friend), ran over and joined us.

"So when you were lying there all dazed, Hannah, did you see any of your angels?" she blurted out.

"Shhh! Not so loud!" I told her. "And…no, I didn't see them. It wasn't like I was dying or anything." Although hardly anyone knows about my angel adventures, Katie and David do. They're super trustworthy, plus it's fun to tell them all my incredible stories.

"I thought for sure you were zapped away on a mission when you were lying there," she said. "Are you *sure* you weren't?"

"Hannah Martin! Katie Chang!" Ms. Montgomery suddenly hollered. "Are we playing ball or gabbing here, girls?" We took the hint and quickly hustled to our positions. I was playing shortstop, and Katie was at first base.

"Thank you, ladies," said Ms. Montgomery as she pulled off her cap and took a deep bow. Sometimes, she can be really dramatic. I think it's kind of funny. One time in mythology class, she acted out stories of Greek gods and goddesses. She was so great! She got into it so much that it was like we were really in Greece witnessing a real goddess perform her magic.

Suddenly, Kyle Jacobson kicked the ball right at me. I grabbed it off the ground and threw it over to Katie at first base just in time. Pretty soon, there were two outs and the Fudge was up.

As I stood in place waiting for the next pitch, I heard a faint siren in the distance. It was coming from beyond Geneva Lake. Then another siren screeched along with it. I hoped they weren't ambulances racing to some boating accident or something. I looked around to see if I could tell where they were going.

"Heads up, Hannah!" yelled Katie. The ball was whizzing right at me. I quickly stuck my leg out and stopped it. I threw it to Katie, and she tagged Jimmy Fudge square on the head.

"Rat boogers!" hollered Fudge.

"You're *out!*" I screamed. I couldn't believe it—our first decent inning. My team started running around, slapping hands. We were beginning to get all fired up.

Fudge getting bonked

"We can take these boys!" one of my teammates yelled.

When I got back to the dugout, I heard the sirens again. This time they were wailing from the opposite direction.

"Where's that coming from?" I asked Katie.

"Where's *what* coming from?" she asked back.

"Those sirens," I said.

"I don't hear anything," she said. I could barely hear her because the high-pitched sound had become so loud.

"Hannah, are you hearing the call of the Sirens?" asked Ms. Montgomery, dangling her arm over my shoulder. I knew she was teasing me, because in her class, we learned about these ancient Greek women called Sirens, who sang in high, beautiful voices. They hypnotized sailors with their songs and lured them to the rocky coast, where their ships crashed.

I didn't tease Ms. Montgomery back, because I didn't know what to say. I felt really weird. I mean, I really was hearing these strange siren noises! I took off my cap and wiped my face with the back of my hand. The sound didn't stop. One minute it was coming from a block behind me. The next minute, it was coming from far away across the lake. It kept getting louder and higher. Then I realized that it *did* sound like singing.

"Hannah?" asked Ms. Montgomery, beginning to look concerned. "Hannah?" I kept hearing over and over, but her voice grew fainter by the second. Pretty soon, all I could hear was the high singing. I felt like I was being hypnotized. I thought of the Sirens enchanting all those sailors as I stared into Ms. Montgomery's green eyes, all weird.

Then the singing stopped.

Somebody else's green eyes were staring back at me!

Chapter 2

A Thousand Cats
and One Angel

The eyes were big, with little flecks of gold in the green. I pulled away from a hairy tan face. It was a cat!

"Meow?" it asked.

"Meow," I answered. That sure was weird! Why was I talking in cat language? "Hello there," I said, correcting myself.

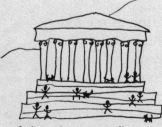

Cats and people at the Parthenon

"Meow," the cat said again as it circled around me affectionately. I was sitting on some old white stone steps, all warmed by the late-afternoon sun. More cats were gathered in little groups here and there. They looked hungry. Lots of tourist-type people were wandering about, stopping to feed them once in a while.

My backpack was lying beside me, which could mean only one thing—I was on an angel mission! I knew exactly where I'd been sent, too, because on my last angel trip, to Paris, my guardian angel Demi had told me where I would be going next. I leapt to my feet.

"Greece!" I cried out loud, twirling around to be sure. Behind me was an enormous ancient building with huge columns, which for sure had to be the Parthenon. Ms. Montgomery would be so jealous if she knew I was in her favorite part of the world, where the Sirens made ships crash and the sun melted Icarus' wax wings, just like she had told us.

Cat in the pack

Down below, I could see a city. Its lights began to twinkle with the coming dusk. I turned to the cat, since he was my only acquaintance. "I'm in Athens, Greece, aren't I?" I asked him. "On top of the famous Acropolis?"

The cat purred very sweetly, staring at me like he wanted me to sit down and pet him. So I did.

"So you're Greek, but you say meow in the same language as the cats where I live do," I said, stroking his head between his ears. He loved it. He jumped into my lap, and it seemed like I'd just made a friend for life.

"You know, Ms. Montgomery says that *Acropolis* means 'high city,' " I told my new friend.

"Is this your home way up here?" I asked as I reached to open my backpack.

When my four angels—Aurora, Lorielle, Lyra, and Demi—whisk me off on these missions, they always make sure I'm well equipped. Every time I go, I have different cool stuff in my backpack that will help me along the way. The cat pawed at the flap of my bag as I opened it. He was as curious as I was.

"Look at all this!" I said as I dumped the contents of my backpack out on the steps. The minute I set the empty pack down, the cat jumped into it, purring happily.

Here's a list of what I found inside my backpack (besides the cat):

Usual stuff:
Angel-language decoder
Flashlight
My journal

Unusual stuff:
Gymnastics handbook
Big lavender T-shirt
(for sleeping?)
Pink-flowered silk dress with
   thin straps (nice!)
Sandals
Zippered case containing scissors, glue, paper,
   toothbrush, and shampoo

some backpack stuff

Greek dictionary
Instant camera
Greek coins (later, I found out they're called
  drachmas)
Map of Athens
Swimsuit

Suddenly, my cat friend pricked up his ears,
shook out his fur, and leapt out of my pack. He
scooted straight up the steps and around a col-
umn like he knew exactly where he was going.
Then he turned back and stared right at me with
those green eyes to see if I was coming.

I still heard the other cats meowing. I looked
up and...whoa! Right from the center of the
Parthenon, a golden light was radiating. It was
growing bigger and brighter by the second.

*Could it actually be a vision of Athena, the Greek
goddess of wisdom?* I thought. I remembered Ms.
Montgomery's story about a gigantic gold-and-
ivory statue of Athena in the Parthenon. But the
statue had been destroyed long ago.

"Hann...ah," I heard. "Hann...nah."

I squinted at the light. Then I glanced all
around me to see if anybody else was hearing and
seeing what I was. No one was! The tourists were
just walking like nothing was happening. But the
cat was staring up at the light. He could see it,
too.

"Hann......nah!" I heard. It was a voice just

like the singing Sirens at the kickball game. Now I knew what it was. It was my angel Lyra, the angel who guides me with music and song! Finally, I could see her, awesome and beautiful, made up of golden light.

"Follow…" I heard her sing. "Follow."

"Follow where?"I asked. I knew this was my chance to find out what my mission was, so I listened hard.

"Follow your friend," she sang.

"What am I looking for, Lyra?" I asked,

A Lyra visit

trying to be as quiet and inconspicuous as possible. "What's my mission?" I whispered.

"Just follow,"I heard. Slowly, Lyra's golden glow grew as huge as the whole Parthenon and dissolved into the sky. Then she was gone. Darn! My angels give me such sketchy clues!

"Excuse me, but who are you talking to?" a tourist behind me suddenly asked. I spun around, and I realized that a small crowd of people were gawking at me like I was a total nut job.

"Ummm…just having a chat with myself," I said. I knew nobody but me had seen Lyra. "I was…I mean…isn't this just an *amazing* place?"

I said, trying to change the subject.

"Well, yes, it certainly is," the tourist answered.

"It just makes you feel like…ummm…like you can actually *see* those old Greek gods and goddesses, doesn't it?"

The man chuckled. "Yes, I guess it does have that effect on some folks," he said. The rest of the crowd started shaking their heads, amused by my enthusiasm.

As soon as the crowd went back to their business, I did exactly as Lyra had told me—I threw my pack over my shoulder, ran up the stairs two at a time, and followed my little green-eyed friend.

Chapter 3

Olympic Dreams

The cat strutted over to a young girl and sat beside her, staring. The girl was smaller than me, with muscular arms and legs and thick black hair tied up in pigtails. She was wearing a blue-and-white gym suit. She was probably around thirteen years old.

"Hi," I said, not knowing what else to say.

"Hello," she answered, barely looking up. I saw that she was reading a note in her hand.

"Meow," said the cat, which made the girl smile. She reached out and gave him a little pat.

"We have a lot of stray cats here in Athens," she said. As she looked up at me, I noticed that her eyes were as golden green as the cat's.

"It sure seems like it," I agreed. "But this guy seems special somehow. I just arrived here, and we're best buddies already."

"He must be part of the welcoming committee," said the girl. "You sound American. Am I right?"

"Yes," I said. "I'm Hannah Martin."

"Welcome to Greece. My name is Alexis," said the girl.

I shook Alexis's hand and then sat down beside her on the white stone steps. "I wonder if this cat has a name," I said.

"How about we call him Catastrophe," Alexis said.

"Catastrophe? You mean, like a really bad accident or something?"

"Yes," said Alexis, crumpling up the paper in her fist.

Catastrophe, me, and Alexis

She looked upset. "Like a terrible event—Catastrophe."

"I'm not sure I like that name," I said. "He seems like a sweet cat to me."

"Oh, it's not him. It's me," said Alexis. "I'm the one who's in the middle of a catastrophe."

"Does it have anything to do with that paper you're holding?" I asked.

Alexis winced at the balled-up paper like there was poison wrapped in it. She tossed it in the air a few times, then pitched it sideways to me. I uncrumpled it. It was a note written in some strange language. At first, it almost looked like the angel code that Lorielle uses when she sends me messages. But there were letters that I'd never seen before.

"Is this Greek?" I asked.

"*Ne,*" she answered. She pronounced it "nay." It sounded like "no."

"No?" I said. "It's not Greek?"

A little reminder

NE = YES
OJI = NO

Alexis giggled. "*Ne* actually means 'yes' in Greek. *Oji* means 'no.'" I immediately knew that I'd get confused every time somebody answered yes or no here!

"So it *is* in Greek," I said. "What does it say?"

"It says: 'You know what happened to Icarus? He fell out of the sky and drowned in the sea,'" Alexis said, looking off into the distance.

"What's that supposed to mean?" I asked.

"I don't know. It's the second strange note I've received since yesterday," said Alexis. "I just got to Athens, and I don't know anybody here except the other gymnasts on my team—"

The nasty note

"You're a gymnast?" I blurted out. "That's so cool!"

"I'm here for the Olympic tryouts," she explained. "I come from Hydra, one of the Greek islands."

"Wow!" I said. "You must be good!"

Alexis smiled. "Well, I'd better be good. I've only been practicing six hours a day for five years." That sounded like a lot to me, so I quickly did the math in my head:

6 hours x 5 years x 365 days.

"That's over ten thousand hours of practice," I said. *How does she have time to eat, or sleep, or have any fun?* I thought.

She looked at me, amazed. "You know, I never figured that out before, Hannah. Ten thousand hours is an incredible amount of time, isn't it?"

"I'll say! So how many girls get picked for the team?" I asked.

"Twenty of us are trying out, but only six will go to the Olympics," she said. "The pressure is on."

"How did they pick the twenty who compete?" I asked.

"We're all on the Greek national team. We've been competing for years. We're actually the first womens' gymnastics team Greece has ever had."

"Oh, I hope you make it, Alexis! You must really want to be in the Olympics."

"Of course I do. It's been my dream since I was a little girl," she said, turning to stare at the paper in my hands. "But I don't understand these notes…"

"Where did you find this?" I asked.

"In the pocket of my team jacket," said Alexis. "Strange, huh?"

"Very strange," I agreed. "You think somebody is trying to scare you?"

"Maybe," she said. "Maybe somebody wants me off the team."

"Why?" I asked.

"How should I know?" she said, looking out into space. "Well, anyway, they won't succeed. I worked too hard to get here." She gave her pigtails a twirl and jumped lightly to her feet. For a second, I thought she was going to do a flip. Then she raced down the steps.

"Come on, Hannah, let's go down into the city," she called back to me. "We'll go to the old part of town—the Plaka. It will take my mind off my worries."

"Well, okay," I agreed.

"The Plaka is full of shops, people, and restaurants. It's a lot of fun."

"Good. It will take my mind off *your* worries, too, Alexis," I teased.

"We can buy some *komboloia*," she suggested.

"Kom-bo-LOY-uh?" I repeated.

"Yes, worry beads. All the men in Greece carry little beads on strings, and they fidget with them to keep from worrying."

"Really? Only the men?"

"Well, there's nothing stopping you or me from getting worry beads. It's just that they are traditionally for men," said Alexis.

"All right, then. Worry beads it is!" I said, hopping onto my feet. "Hey! What about our furry friend, Catastrophe?"

"He'll be fine," said Alexis. "He knows how to get his next meal from the tourists."

I turned to wave good-bye to Catastrophe, but he was already loping back to the Parthenon with his tail in the air.

As we headed down the steps, I stuck the crumpled note in my pocket. I had a feeling that I might be needing it...

Chapter 4

Peril in the Plaka

I stared at the beautiful lights of Athens as Alexis and I strolled down the winding road toward the Plaka.

"What time is it?" I asked Alexis.

"Eight," she answered. "I've got to be back at the dorm by nine-thirty. Coach's orders."

"Do all the gymnasts stay in the same place?" I asked.

"The guys' team stays in one dorm, and we stay in another. The girls room together, eat together, practice together…"

"And then you compete against each other," I said. It sounded kind of awkward to me—being friends but wanting to beat each other, too. If a game of kickball at home was so competitive, I couldn't imagine Olympic tryouts!

"Yes. And you...where are you staying, Hannah?" she asked.

"Uh...I'm not actually sure," I said. I knew my angels would help me figure that out, but I didn't know what to tell Alexis. "I mean...my friends need to let me know." *Friends? I thought. What friends? Catastrophe and his little cat buddies at the Acropolis?*

Alexis wrapped her arm through mine as we got to the bottom of the hill. "Stay with us in the dorm room," she said. "It would be fun to have a visitor!"

"Okay, thanks a lot," I said. *Great! There's one problem taken care of.* My next challenge was to figure out what my mission was. I knew it had something to do with Alexis and those nasty notes, but that was all I'd figured out so far.

The Plaka was really cool. It had these narrow streets that went up and down hills. Cars were honking, people were hurrying, and vendors were selling pottery, brass, rugs, and embroidered clothes. At one shop, there were strings and strings of colorful beads on chains.

"Look at all those bracelets!" I said.

"They're not bracelets," said Alexis. "They're the worry beads I was talking about. Which are your favorites?"

I picked out some cloudy sky-blue beads and started flipping them over in my fingers like Alexis had said the men do. But they didn't do much—they sort of just flipped over once and then sat there in the palm of my hand.

"Here, I'll show you," said Alexis, using her thumb to flip the beads over and between her fingers. I tried again, but I still felt like a klutz.

Just then, we heard loud shouting coming  from the shop next to us. A man in a captain's hat and white clothes was arguing with a vendor. He seemed to have an entourage with him—three beautiful women and a young man in a black cap.

"What's he saying?" I asked Alexis.

In the plaka

"He thinks the vendor cheated his friend on a rug he bought yesterday. And he's *very* angry," she answered.

"I can see that," I said. I don't really like yelling. It makes me all nervous and squirmy, so I concentrated on flipping my worry beads.

Alexis grabbed my arm and steered me away. "That man is Helena's dad—Helena is one of the girls on the Greek gymnastics team," she whispered. "I think he's some kind of important businessman. He has a huge yacht, and I heard that he even owns an island."

I glanced back over my shoulder. "Well, he seems pretty rude, too," I said. By now, this guy was *really* hollering.

"He's probably used to getting his way," said Alexis. "Come on, let's go."

We were heading deeper into the Plaka when we were jostled next to a vendor's stand. All of a sudden, the weirdest thing happened—a huge fishnet came hurtling down from the roof of the building we were standing next to.

"Watch out, Alexis!" I yelled. But it was too late. The net tumbled right on top of us. We were totally tangled up inside! We started flailing around like two trapped fish caught in the ropes.

Hannahfish and friend

"Help!" I shouted, struggling to get untangled from the net. "Somebody get this thing off us!"

Alexis was yelling in Greek, so I couldn't understand a word of it. But clearly, she wanted out, too. The vendor was hollering and looking up at the roof, trying to figure out where the fishnet had come from. He and Alexis had a quick discussion in Greek. I could tell from the look in Alexis's eyes that she suspected somebody had thrown the net down specifically to land on her. I wondered if somebody really *was* out to scare her into failing the tryouts.

Just then, Helena's dad and his three women friends came rushing over.

"Alexis!" said Helena's dad. "Are you hurt?"

"What happened?" asked one of the women. She was all decked out in white silky clothes and had shiny red nails. She reeked of exotic flowers. I noticed that she didn't touch the net, and neither did Helena's father. He started giving orders to people around him, like he was the boss or something. Every time he pointed a finger, somebody obeyed and did what he told them to do.

Pretty soon, Alexis and I were out of the net and being helped to our feet.

"It's like he has superpowers," I whispered to Alexis. "He snaps his fingers and everybody jumps."

"I told you—he's a very powerful man," she said.

Helena's dad shook my hand warmly. "I'm Xenos," he said. (It sounded like ZEE-noss.) "Spelled with an X."

"I'm Hannah," I said. "Spelled with an H."

He chuckled at my little joke and wrapped his arm around Alexis's shoulder. "Alexis, come. Let me take you and your friend for something to eat. What a terrible trial you've just had. This is definitely *not* a good way to start a visit to our wonderful city of Athens."

He said something in Greek to the three women, and they immediately marched off. It was like he was a captain dismissing his soldiers. So I decided that Captain X was a good nickname for this guy.

Captain X put a gigantic arm gently around each of us and led us to an outdoor café. A waiter appeared before we even sat down.

"We will speak English!" Captain X announced with bravado. "We have a friend from the United States with us tonight!"

The waiter bowed. "Yes, sir, Mr. Xenos," he said. "What can I get for you?"

"Three lemonades," said Captain X, without even asking us what we wanted. Poor Helena, whoever she was! I couldn't imagine this guy being *my* dad—we'd be fighting all the time. It's not that I didn't want lemonade, but I do like to be asked first, you know?

"Anchovies, spinach pies, olives, some cheese," Captain X added. *Anchovies?* For sure, I like to be asked first!

"So, Alexis, how did tryouts go today?" he asked. He leaned forward to listen to Alexis as if she were the only person in the Plaka.

As they talked about the tryouts, the younger man in the black cap reappeared and joined us. I figured that he was the one who had been cheated on the rug.

"Paolo!" Captain X greeted him. "You have returned!"

"Yes, sir," said Paolo. "I took care of the errand you asked me to do."

"Good!" said Captain X. "Meet my young friends Alexis and Hannah."

"*Ti kanate?*" Paolo asked us. (It sounded like tee-KON-uh-tay.)

"We're just fine," answered Alexis in English. By the way, Paolo was a major MacCutie, as Katie would say. He had twinkling dark eyes and a big, friendly white-toothed smile. He looked like he was waiting to crack a joke.

"I like your hat," I told him as we shook hands.

"Oh, it's just a fisherman's cap. You'll see a lot of these in Greece," he said.

Before Paolo could sit down, the captain waved his hands theatrically.

"*Parakalo*, Paolo. Please go buy Hannah a fisherman's cap just like yours," Captain X said. He reached into his pocket and handed Paolo some cash.

"When in Greece," the captain said to me, winking, "you want to dress like a Greek!"

I began to object. "But I didn't mean for you to buy me—"

"Nonsense," Captain X interrupted. "I insist! *Parakalo*, Paolo!"

As Paolo hurried off, the captain turned his black eyes and his full attention to me.

"So, Hannah, you and Alexis are long-lost friends?" he asked.

"Not yet," I said, laughing. "We actually just met."

"You did?" he said, seeming surprised. "So you're here vacationing?"

"Ummm...in a way," I said. "I've always wanted to see the Acropolis."

"You are very young to be wandering the city alone," he said, raising his bushy eyebrows.

"Your parents must trust you very much!"

"Of course they do," I replied, a little miffed.

"Are you also a gymnast?"

"No way," I said. He was asking me so many questions that I couldn't even drink my lemonade. In two minutes, Captain X knew that I live in Geneva, Wisconsin, that lavender is my favorite color, that my birthday is April Fools' Day, that my mom's a computer programmer and my dad is a veterinarian, and that I have a dog named Frank! I started to get a little annoyed by his prying. So I turned the tables on him.

"So what about you, Mr. Xenos?" I said. And then I asked him as many questions as he'd just asked me.

Pretty soon, I learned that Helena is his only daughter, his wife died two years ago and he is still heartbroken about it, he has a few homes in Greece, Paolo is a deck hand on board his yacht—which is named *Helena*—his business is too complicated to explain, and anyway, he preferred to talk about more enjoyable things.

"Like what?" I pried.

"Like Athens, or the history of Greece, or music, or dancing…"

"Dancing!" cried Alexis, interrupting. "Yes, Hannah, you have to learn to dance *syrtaki* while you're in Greece!" (It sounded like soor-TOCK-ee).

"Absolutely!" Captain X agreed. "It's one of our traditional Greek dances."

"Great!" I said. If I could learn an Irish jig on

my angel adventure with Molly Ryan, I figured that I could certainly learn a Greek dance, too.

I was just reaching for my first taste of spinach pie when Alexis suddenly leapt to her feet.

"Oh my goodness! It's nine!" she cried. "I've got to go! Coach Gretel will be furious with me if I'm late!"

"She'll have her leotards all in a knot!" teased Paolo, who walked up at that very moment. He had bought not *one* fisherman's cap, but *two*.

Paolo with two caps

"One for each of you!" he said, plopping one on each of our heads.

"Beautiful!" commented Captain X, his arms outspread.

"Thank you so much!" I said, grabbing my backpack and a handful of olives.

"*Ne, efharisto!*" said Alexis. (It sounded like eff-ha-ree-STO.)

"We must meet again soon, and dance *syrtaki*," Captain X called after us.

Alexis and I waved back to them as we sped off, winding our way out of the crowd and through the Plaka.

Chapter 5

Rope Trick

We were racing through the Plaka when suddenly the whole Acropolis lit up. The ancient buildings turned a bright, luminous yellow, and the Parthenon looked like it was made of gold!

I stopped in my tracks, wide-eyed. "It's my angels!" I gasped.

Alexis turned and gave me a weird look. "No, it's a sound-and-light show," she said. "The Acropolis lights up every night at nine."

"Oh," I said in a small voice, realizing I'd just put my foot in my mouth.

"Did you say you thought your *angels* lit it up?" Alexis asked. From the look on her face, I could tell she definitely thought I was a little loopy.

"Ummm...well, yes...silly me!" I stammered.

"I have no idea why that came out of my mouth!"

Alexis gave me a suspicious sideways glance. "Let's go, okay, Hannah?"

We hurried through the dark, narrow streets toward a building that looked like a school. Alexis stopped next to a wall that surrounded the entire building.

"These are the dorms where we're staying," she whispered. "We're not supposed to have overnight visitors, so we have to figure out a way to sneak you in."

It wasn't exactly the first time I'd done something risky, but I got a little nervous, anyway. If we got caught and they kicked me out, I would wind up sleeping with Catastrophe and his pals at the Acropolis. I guess I could think of worse places to sleep (like in the Fudge's house!).

Me, Catastrophe, and pals

"Where exactly is your room?" I asked.

Alexis pointed to a third-floor window with a balcony. "That's it. Room 318," she said. "What I'll do is go in the front door, get to my room, and lower a rope for you to climb up."

I gulped, looking at how high above the ground the window was.

"Lower a rope?" I squeaked.

"Don't worry, it's not that high," Alexis said. "I'm sure you can climb it, Hannah."

"I have a better idea," I said. "Since *you're* the gymnast, how about *I* walk in the front door, and I lower a rope for *you?*" I suggested.

"That's fine," said Alexis. She handed me her pass card, with her picture on it. The photo was so small that you couldn't really tell I wasn't her.

"The security person doesn't know me personally, so he'll just let you in with the pass," said Alexis. "Come this way. I'll have my roommates lower the rope and I'll go up it first. Then I'll let you in when you get to the room," she said.

Alexis directed me through an entryway in the wall. Then we walked across the lawn until we were under her window.

"Sophia! Maria!" Alexis called up to the window. Suddenly, two girls peeked out onto the little balcony.

"Alexis!" said one girl in a raspy whisper. "You better get your butt up here before Coach Gretel checks on us. You're gonna be late!"

"I'm coming," said Alexis. "And we have a visitor for the evening. Her name's Hannah." I waved up at the girls, and they waved back.

"Hi, Hannah," said one girl. "But how will she get in here?"

"She's coming in the front with my pass, and I'm climbing up!" called Alexis. "Toss me the rope." I figured that these girls must sneak in and out behind the coach's back all the time, because the next thing I knew, a rope came tumbling down from above. It was like clockwork.

"Go on, Hannah, hurry!" called Alexis as she started shinnying up the rope. She was moving fast, and the rope didn't even have knots in it to hold on to. "I'll meet you in Room 318!"

"Okay!" I said, heading for the front door. I walked in and flashed my pass to the security guard like I knew what I was doing. I made sure not to open my mouth because I was supposed to be Greek. He let me go by without a problem. I hurried up the stairs and down the hall to Room 318, where Alexis was already waiting at the door.

"You're fast," I said. The three girls hustled me in and closed the door. Sophia and Maria were already in their pj's.

"Quick, change into your pajamas before Coach gets here!" Sophia told Alexis.

I figured that I might as well change, too. After all, this was the first time my angels had actually supplied me with a nightshirt, a toothbrush, and shampoo. I wonder why it's taken them so long to figure out that after days of not having any bathroom stuff, us humans can get pretty funky. I guess it's because they're angels and they don't have to worry about things like dusty hair and nasty breath. Lucky them.

Anyway, I got all comfy and joined Sophia, Maria, and Alexis in a little circle on the floor. Sophia was telling tales about the pranks she had played at gym camp the summer before. She seemed like one of those girls who can be pretty catty if you don't watch out.

"And remember the itching powder we put in the chalk?" she howled.

Alexis turned to me. "We have to rub our hands in chalk so we won't slip on the parallel bars," she explained.

"So just before Alexis used the chalk, we loaded it with itching powder," said Sophia.

"And I completely lost my grip," said Alexis. "My hands got so itchy that I couldn't hold on to the bars."

"You were so mad!" said Sophia, falling backward because she was laughing so hard.

"It was just a little joke, Alexis. We really didn't mean anything by it," Maria said. It seemed to me that Maria was Sophia's sidekick. But she appeared to be very sweet. "Really, Alexis," she said sincerely.

"I know, Maria," said Alexis, smiling. "Don't worry, I'm not mad anymore."

"Shhh!" cried Sophia suddenly. "I think I hear Coach Gretel!"

The three girls dove for their beds. They

pulled up the covers and pretended to be sleeping.

"Hannah, you've got to hide!" whispered Alexis. I quickly checked around in a panic, but I couldn't see anyplace to go.

"The balcony!" hissed Maria. I could hear the coach's footsteps outside the door to the hall. I dove through the open door onto the balcony just as Coach Gretel called, "Bed check!" I gingerly slipped off to the side, out of sight. As I plastered myself against the wall, I heard a loud grunt. It sounded like it was right by my feet! I froze. *What was that?* I thought, totally terrified. I mean, here I was, at least thirty feet off the ground on this tiny balcony, in the dark, in a foreign country. And now, on top of it all, I was hearing strange grunts? Somehow, I had managed to get myself into *another* interesting situation, to say the least.

"Lights out, girls!" I heard Coach Gretel say in a thick German accent. "Get a good sleep for practice tomorrow." She flipped off the bedroom light, so now it was even darker on the balcony.

"Who's there?" I whispered into the dark. I looked down and saw the shadow of a hand right next to my foot. Then another shadowy hand. Somebody was climbing up the rope—onto the balcony!

Chapter 6

Who Goes There?

What should I do? I wondered, totally freaked out. *Should I scream so Coach Gretel hears me and comes out to help?* But the problem with that was if she found me on the balcony, the girls would be in big trouble. Not to mention that I'd be sleeping with the stray cats.

Should I wait until Coach Gretel leaves and then scream? I thought. But depending on who this shadow was, I might not have time to wait. I didn't know what to do, so I just held my breath, terrified.

"Good night, girls," I heard Coach Gretel say.

"Good night, Coach Gretel," said the girls.

Just then, one of the shadowy hands grabbed my ankle. I saw a head appearing over the edge of the balcony. I took a deep breath. I picked up my foot and slammed the hand off my ankle with all my might.

"Ouch!" yelled a guy's voice as a hand grabbed my other ankle.

I heard the door close inside the dorm room. "Alexis!" I hollered as I slammed my foot down on the guy's other hand. He let out a moan and grabbed the balcony railing with both hands.

"You're going to break all the bones in my body!" the guy howled in pain.

"Are you all right, Hannah? Who's out there?" cried Alexis, racing outside onto the balcony.

"Oh, it's just Costas!" said Sophia, joining us.

"You know this guy?" I asked, backing off.

"He's a friend of Sophia's," whispered Maria.

"I'm surprised Hannah didn't kick you all the way down to the street, Costas!" Sophia scolded, shaking her head. "You know that you shouldn't be sneaking up here this late. This is when Coach Gretel does her room check, you jerk!"

"Sorry, Sophia," Costas said sheepishly, pulling himself up onto the balcony and rubbing his hands. He was short and thin with very curly black hair. He looked like a gymnast himself. He ran his finger gently across Sophia's cheek. "I'm really sorry. I am."

Sophia pushed his hand away. "Costas!" she

hissed. "Do you have any idea how bad this is?"

"What were you doing grabbing my ankles?" I said. I figured that I might as well get my two cents in. "You scared me to death!"

"And you could get me disqualified from the tryouts!" added Sophia.

"I don't want to do that," said Costas. He started to get all flirty and pouty. He ran his finger around Sophia's ear. "I just had to see you, and the rope was out there, so—"

"I should have pulled it up behind me," Alexis interrupted.

Sophia swatted Costas's hand away again. "You have to go now, Costas. I'll see you after practice tomorrow."

All three girls were standing there with their hands on their hips, waiting for Costas to shinny back down the rope. He hung his head like an injured puppy dog.

"Okay, Sophia. Tomorrow at three-thirty." He flung one leg after the other over the railing and started down the rope. "I miss you already!" he called.

Sophia started to giggle. "Isn't he sweet?" she said, sparkly after he left. We started giggling, so we moved into the room, where Costas wouldn't hear.

"So is he your new boyfriend, Sophia?" asked Maria.

"Maybe," said Sophia. "I'm thinking about it."

She wrapped her arms behind her knees and flipped over backward, landing squarely on her feet. My mouth fell wide open in amazement.

"How do you do that?" I asked.

"She's in *love*," teased Maria. "Love can make you do *anything*."

Just then, we heard footsteps coming down the hall. Everybody dove into their beds and shut their eyes. I took a giant leap back out onto the balcony before Coach Gretel poked her head in.

Sophia in love

It was quiet on the balcony now. Once Coach Gretel left, I pulled up the rope and untied it from the railing. It was a beautiful night, and the sky was full of stars. I stuck my head into the room. "You don't think Costas will be coming back, do you?" I asked.

"Not a chance," whispered Maria. "Sophia scared him away."

"Then I'm sleeping on the balcony tonight," I said. "It's safe out here, isn't it?"

"Sure," said Alexis as she threw me a sleeping bag. I said good night and then grabbed my backpack. I sat on the sleeping bag and pulled out a few things—my journal, my flashlight, and the crumpled note from my pocket. Then I began writing some notes about my angel trip so far:

My angel trip notes:

Alexis, the youngest member of the team, just arrives in Athens and receives two nasty notes. Then a fishnet falls on her head (and mine!) in the Plaka. I think I agree with Alexis—somebody is trying to frighten her out of the Olympic trials. But who? And why?

Just then, this weird thing happened that's happened only once before, on my angel mission in Ireland. My hand started writing all by itself! Lorielle was sending me a message! My pen moved right along the page, and my hand followed. When Lori's message was complete, it read:

△⌇⚬✋ ♂⟜◎☆ ⅏☆↑ △⌇⚬♡ö ⌇⟜↑◎⚲

It was in angel code! So now if anybody got ahold of my journal and tried to read Lori's warning, they wouldn't be able to. I pulled out my decoder and figured out what the message said.

"I've met my match?" I said to myself, totally confused. "What do you mean, Lori?" I asked. "Do you mean that I already know who it is? Have I already met the person who is trying to sabotage Alexis?"

An angel message

I waited for Lori to write me an answer. But my pen was still. I waited a few seconds longer. Nothing. So I decided to write my question down, in case these angels of mine couldn't hear me for some reason.

"Do I already know the person who is trying to hurt Alexis?" I wrote.

Gradually, from far in the distance, I began to hear the same high-pitched singing that I had heard at the Geneva Lake Festival. This time, I knew it wasn't the Sirens. The song grew louder and louder until I clearly heard Lyra's words:

Yes...you...do.

Chapter 7

Practice Makes Perfect

I couldn't believe that I was standing out in front of the dorms waiting for a shuttle bus at six-thirty A.M. And I'd already eaten breakfast! I had no idea how these girls did this every morning—I was still half asleep.

"You get up at five-thirty *every* morning?" I asked Maria.

Maria groaned back and nodded a little. Well, I guess she wasn't exactly perky at this hour, either.

It didn't help matters much that I'd had a fit-ful sleep the night before. First of all, it turned chilly out on the balcony, and I couldn't help but think about

Cat dreaming

Catastrophe and all his stray-cat buddies up on the Acropolis. I was wishing that I could give each of them a blanket, a little milk, and a cozy place to sleep. But what really kept me awake was the angel message. *I already knew the person who was tormenting Alexis?* But I hadn't even met that many people yet. I figured that I should tell Alexis about this today and see what she thought.

Just then, Coach Gretel stepped out the door. It was the first I'd seen of her. She looked just like a grown-up version of Hansel's sister, blond braids and all. And wouldn't you know it, she walked straight up to me.

"Hello," she said cheerfully. "And who might you be?"

"I'm Hannah," I said. "I'm a friend of Alexis. I was hoping that I could please watch Alexis practice a little?" I said, squirming a bit.

"I'm glad you've checked with me first," said Coach Gretel. "My girls are getting photos taken this morning, so you can stay until then."

"Thank you!" I said.

"But you'll have to leave right after the photo shoot," she said firmly. "The girls must focus on their practice. We keep distractions to a minimum."

"Okay," I agreed. The shuttle bus pulled up, and I hopped on with the team.

When we got to the gym, the girls were all business. They started with their warm-ups while

I sat on the side watching. They took turns on each piece of equipment. Alexis told me there are four events: the balance beam, tumbling, the uneven parallel bars, and vaulting. For short, they call them beam, floor, bars, and vault.

Alexis started with tumbling. Tumbling is the somersaulting and other stuff you do on the floor. I thought I'd get in a little stretching myself, so I tried to do the splits that Alexis was doing. No way! I got about six inches from the ground, and my thighs began to burn so bad that I lost my balance. I decided I'd be a better spectator than a gymnast, so I took a seat again.

Alexis did some handstand pirouettes, front aerials, and roundoffs. Wow, doesn't it sound like I know what I'm talking about? Well, that's because I checked out the gymnastics handbook that my angels had sent along. It turned out to be really helpful! Each of those exercises is called a trick. Alexis told me that the tricks aren't so hard by themselves. But you have to put a few tricks together to make up a tumbling pass. And then you have to put

A gymnast

Not a gymnast

two or three passes together to make up a full routine. Now *that* sounds pretty hard.

Anyway, you should have seen Alexis go. She was awesome! I started to wonder who might be trying to scare her off the team. So I pulled out my journal.

First, I read over what I'd written the night before. Then I listed every person I'd met in Greece by the time I got Lori's message:

Alexis herself (highly unlikely)

A few tourists (very doubtful)

Captain X

His three women friends (but I didn't really meet them, so I wondered if they even counted)

Paolo

Sophia

Maria

Costas

Coach Gretel

(Oh, and Catastrophe, just in case he was a magic
  shape-shifter or something)

Then I went into my secret-spy mode and eyeballed each of Alexis's teammates to see if I
noticed anything suspicious. Of course, in a way,
they could *all* look suspicious because they all
were competing against each other for a spot on
the Olympic team.

Coach Gretel blew her whistle. "Okay, take a
break, girls," she yelled. "Time for photos!"

Everybody gathered together and posed for a
team photo on the parallel bars. They were all in
their blue-and-white Greek team outfits. I wanted
a souvenir, so I pulled out the camera my angels
sent and shot a quick picture, too.

"This is very kind of Mr. Xenos to take pictures of the team," Coach Gretel told the photographer. "Please make sure to thank him for me
once again."

"It's nothing," said the photographer. "We'll
have proofs back to the girls tomorrow."

"Great!" she said.

One by one, each of the girls got an individual
shot taken. Alexis looked like a star to me, a total
future Olympian. I had a great idea for what I'd

do when her photo came back—sort of a little present for her. "Okay, Hannah," said Coach Gretel, nodding at me. "See you at four-thirty for the shuttle." I knew she meant it was time for me to leave. So I tucked my journal and camera into my backpack and scooted out the door.

Chapter 8

Very Good Secret

I left the gym and stepped out into the bright, sunny day. I put on my new fisherman's cap and looked at the map of Athens that my angels had packed for me. I decided to start exploring back at the Parthenon, since everything was easy to find from there. And who knew? Maybe Lyra would be hanging out there with another clue for me.

When I got to the Acropolis, guess who showed up? None other than my favorite little Catastrophe.

"Hey, buddy!" I said as he circled my legs. My dad says that's the way cats kiss people. I sat down on the steps, and Catastrophe curled into my lap, his green eyes staring up at me. He looked just like a mini tiger, right out of the jungle.

Catastrophe the tiger

"So who's being mean to Alexis?" I asked Catastrophe as I rubbed his soft neck. "Who tossed that net over us yesterday?"

"A net? You mean the one in the Plaka?" said a voice behind me.

I spun around. Catastrophe let out a loud hiss, leapt up, and took off like a shot.

"Paolo," I said. "You surprised me."

"You surprised me, too," he replied. "I thought you might be at practice with Alexis."

"Coach Gretel made me leave. The gymnasts have to focus and be serious. Did you know they practice six hours a day?" I said.

He wiped his brow. "Whew! That's hard work, isn't it? Almost as hard as being the deck hand on a ship," he said, a bit sarcastically.

"Aren't you working today, Paolo?" I asked, looking around for Catastrophe. But the cat was nowhere to be seen.

"I *am* working," he said. "I'm running errands for Mr. Xenos. I'm just taking a coffee break at the moment." Paolo held up his steaming paper cup.

"Say, Hannah, do you want to join me?" he asked. "I can show you a little of Athens while I make my stops."

I ran through the list of suspects in my head. Paolo seemed safe enough, but the way I saw it, nobody could be totally trusted. Not yet, anyway. But maybe I'd get some clues if I hung around with him for a few hours.

"Sure, Paolo," I said. "Why not?"

"*Kala*," he said. "That means 'good' in Greek."

We trotted down the massive steps and hopped on his motorbike.

"Don't we need helmets for this?" I asked. "At home, there are laws that say—"

"There are no laws like that in Greece," he interrupted as he revved the motor. "I don't even know if they sell helmets in the stores here. So hang on to your hat!" Suddenly, we were winding down the hill, through the Plaka, past a big square that had fancy glass-and-steel buildings around it.

"Constitution Square," Paolo hollered back to me over the whistling wind. "We're almost at our first stop." He soon pulled to the curb by a party supply store and hopped off the motorbike.

"We'll get our balloons and streamers here," he said.

"Balloons and streamers? For what?" I asked, following him toward the shop.

He stopped and leaned next to me. "Can you keep a secret?" he asked.

"Depends on what the secret is," I said. "Is it a good secret or a bad secret?"

"It is *poli kala*," he said.

"Po-LEE ka-LA?" I repeated. "What does that mean?"

"It means good...very good!" said Paolo, winking at me with a big smile. (Geez, I had almost forgotten what a MacCutie he was.)

"In that case, yes, I can keep a secret," I said.

Paolo checked around to see that no one was listening. Then he leaned closer and pulled my cap off my head. He held it next to my ear to muffle the sound of his voice. "Mr. Xenos is planning a big party on his private yacht," he whispered. "All the girls on Helena's team will be invited. An elegant bash!" He stepped back and raised both eyebrows to emphasize just how impressed he thought I should be.

"Cool!" I said. And you know what? I *was* impressed! It sounded like a lot of fun.

Paolo held my hat next to my ear again. "Do you want to go to the party?"

"Of course!" I nearly shouted. "When is it?"

"Tonight."

"*Tonight?*" I repeated.

"It's a very last-minute thing," said Paolo. "But Mr. Xenos felt this was the only night it would work."

"So the whole team is invited?" I asked.

"*Ne*. And since you're helping me do the shopping, I will add your name to our guest list," Paolo said emphatically, as if he was giving me a great gift. He pulled a little black book out of his pocket and jotted something in it.

"Hannah Martin, you are now officially on the guest list!" he announced with a dramatic stroke of his pen. "You'll get your invitation tonight along with the other girls."

I clapped my hands together. A private yacht, a big party—this was awesome!

"But remember, it's a secret!" he said as he set the cap back on my head with a big smile. "We want the girls to be surprised!"

"I won't say a word!" I assured him.

"All right, let's go get those balloons!" Paolo said enthusiastically.

By the time we were done, I couldn't believe how many balloons, streamers, packs of glitter, and flowers we had bought. The flowers were all pale blue and white, just like the Greek team's colors (my idea!). They looked really nice, if I do say so myself. Then we zoomed off to the market and ordered huge amounts of food, all to be delivered to Captain X's yacht later in the day. I never saw so much money being spent in my whole life.

At noon, we stopped at the National Gardens. We bought *souvlaki* from a street vendor. *Souvlaki* is what we call gyros at home—you know, meat and tomatoes and yogurt, all wrapped up in pita bread. Then we sat on a bench for a little picnic. Talk about a lot of cats! There were even more wandering around the gardens than up on the Acropolis.

"I feel really bad for these cats," I told Paolo. "Don't they have any place to live?"

"No, but they have a lot of food, since the

tourists are always feeding them," said Paolo.

"But still," I objected, "if I were a cat, I'd want a place to call home."

"They're only animals, Hannah," Paolo said.

Well, I for sure didn't like that. I immediately thought of my dad. He's a veterinarian, so he'd hate to see all these homeless cats. And I'm like him—I'd take them all home with me if I could. But my mom would kill me. She thinks my dad and I would turn our house into a huge, stinky zoo if we had our way: gorillas, toucans, snakes— an entire rain forest. You know, I think she's probably right.

Paolo and I then scooted around Athens for a couple more errands. We mailed letters and bought CD's. I got to see some awesome ancient ruins along the way, too. At four-thirty, Paolo dropped me back at the gym.

"Now, don't let the cat out of the bag," he reminded me, raising his finger to his lips.

I gave him a thumbs-up. I certainly would keep the secret about the party. But I had learned a more important secret while I was with Paolo—a secret that I'd Paolo's little black book have to write down in my journal as a clue. Paolo had written my full name—Hannah Martin—in his little black book.

But I'd never told him what my last name is. And I hadn't told Captain X, either.

Chapter 9

You're Invited...Where?

Alexis was shaking when she came out of the gym. It was pretty obvious that something was really bothering her, and I had a feeling it was more than just having had a bad practice. We boarded the shuttle bus to go back to the dorm, and she barely said one word the whole trip.

"Let's go someplace where we can talk, Hannah," she whispered as we got off the shuttle bus. As the rest of the kids went back to the dorms, Alexis and I caught a bus headed toward the Acropolis.

"Do you have any *drachmas*?" Alexis asked as we boarded. She held out some coins in her hand, so I figured that *drachmas* were Greek money.

"I think so," I said, fishing out a few of the coins my angels had packed for me. I stared at them in the palm of my hand, baffled.

"But I have no idea how much I need," I said.

"Here, I'll show you," said Alexis, taking a few coins to pay the driver.

We got off the bus at a part of the Acropolis different from where we had been before. This time, we were down below the Parthenon. I followed Alexis to a huge circle of ancient rocks that looked a lot like bleachers in a gym. In the center was a flat area, like a stage.

"This is the amphitheater," said Alexis. "They used to perform plays here centuries ago."

This would be Ms. Montgomery's all-time favorite spot on planet Earth, I thought. I was going to tell Alexis about my mythology teacher, but I could see that she was too stressed out to enjoy that type of conversation.

Me and Alexis at the amphitheater

No one else was around, so we sat down on the old rocky theater seats. Alexis reached into her pocket and pulled out a note.

"I found this stuck in the door of my locker when I finished practice," she said, passing it over to me. It looked just like the other note—black ink on white paper, written in Greek.

"What does it say?" I asked.

"'You know what happened to the Winged Victory? She lost her head,'" Alexis read.

"I don't understand," I said.

"They are talking about a famous statue of

Nike," she explained. "It's called the Winged Victory."

"Nike...like the shoes?" I asked.

"Yes. Nike was the goddess of victory. The statue is ancient. She has beautiful wings but no head. It broke off and was lost years ago."

"Alexis, you don't think somebody is really threatening to hurt...or even *kill* you...," I whispered.

"I have no idea," she said.

"Well, one thing's for sure," I continued. "Somebody wants you out of the Olympic trials."

"It has to be one of my teammates," she said. "They're the only ones who know which locker is mine."

I reached into my backpack and pulled out my journal.

"I made a list of possible suspects," I told her. "Whoever is threatening you has to be someone I met yesterday."

"How do you know that?" asked Alexis.

"Ummm, I just know it," I said weakly. "I'm really sure about that—don't ask me why. Just call it intuition."

Alexis raised her eyebrows, surprised. "Is this like when you thought angels lit up the Parthenon last night?" she asked.

I laughed, trying to sound natural, but it came out really forced. "Well, not exactly. That was silly of me. But this I know—the person we're after is on this list right here in my journal. Trust me."

Alexis leaned over and checked out my journal.

"Only two of my teammates are listed here," she said, shocked. "Sophia and Maria!"

"Yes," I said.

"No!" she countered. "They're my roommates. I trust them. I mean, Sophia is bossy and hard to get along with sometimes, but that doesn't mean she's..."

"What?" I asked.

"Hannah, why would they be trying to knock me out of competition?"

"I've been thinking about this, Alexis," I said. "Is it possible that if you get chosen for the team, one of them could be eliminated?"

"Of course that's possible," she said, leaping to her feet. "But that's true for every girl on the team. When one of us is picked, it means another girl *wasn't* picked."

"How well do you know Sophia?" I asked. I wasn't so concerned about Maria. She may have acted like Sophia's shadow, but she also seemed very nice and sincere.

"I've been on the Greek national team for three years. Since I was ten," she said. Suddenly, she did two cartwheels down the old steps and landed on the stage. She acted like there was nothing to it.

"But would you call Sophia a *true* friend?" I

asked, walking down the steps so I wouldn't have to shout at her.

"I know both Sophia and Maria well as teammates," she answered. "But, no, they're not my best friends..."

"Then I think you should be careful with them until we know more about these notes," I suggested.

Alexis started twirling around and around like a ballerina in the middle of the stage. Talk about nervous energy! "I *hate* this!" she moaned. "I wish these notes would just go away."

"I know how upset you must be, Alexis. This a terrible situation to be in. So let me help you out," I said.

"Maybe we should go to the police," she replied.

"Do you think they'd take these notes seriously?" I asked.

"No," said Alexis. "We don't have enough evidence," she added, looking down at the ground. "I also thought of going to Coach Gretel, but she'll just read the notes out loud in front of the team or something. That won't help."

"Besides," I said, "what if Coach Gretel has something to do with all this?"

"My coach?" Alexis asked, looking angry. "No way! She's definitely not involved," she said. "That would make no sense at all."

"Well, then, let's figure this out together," I suggested.

Alexis nodded, and we sat down with my list. I told her about Paolo and how I thought it was strange that he knew my last name. Alexis told me that the little pranks Sophia plays are sometimes pretty mean. I made notes about everything, and then we headed back to the dorms.

On the bulletin board in the hall, the coach had posted a big notice: PRACTICE STARTS AT 10:00 A.M. TOMORROW.

"What's that about?" asked Alexis. "How come it's so late?"

I decided to keep my promise to Paolo and not say a word. But as soon as we stepped into our room, Alexis found out, anyway. Sophia and Maria were jumping around, hugging each other. Each had a big envelope in her hands.

"Alexis! Hannah!" they yelled. "These are for you!"

We opened our envelopes. Silver glitter fell out all over the place. I acted all surprised to find a balloon and my invitation inside. Alexis began to read her invitation.

"You are invited to a grand party at...*where?*" she shouted when she came to the part about the yacht.

"On Helena's yacht!" cried Maria, jumping for joy.

"For a private party!" Sophia added, leaping up in the air and touching her toes.

"Wow! It says to dress up and bring a swim-suit," I said.

"This is the nicest note I've gotten in a long time," said Alexis, glancing toward me. I watched the other girls for a reaction to her comment. But they were still screaming and jumping up and down, so I joined in. All four of us danced around until Alexis hollered.

"Hold everything!" she screamed. She looked a little upset. I had no idea what was bothering her.

We stopped and waited. Slowly, the corners of Alexis's mouth rose into a big smile. "We have to get down to business, ladies," she said enthusiastically. "Let's talk about what we're wearing on our cruise!"

Chapter 10

The Ship Trip

Now that I knew we had to get dressed up for a fancy party on a big yacht, I realized why my angels had left me the sandals and the pink flowered sundress in my backpack. I quickly pulled them out for the girls to see.

"How's this?" I asked, holding the dress high in the air.

Everyone agreed it was awesome. I quickly headed down the hall to take a shower. We all shared one huge bathroom with a bunch of showers, sinks, and mirrors. Girls were running around everywhere, all excited. I guess when gymnasts are excited, they do handstands and cartwheels and stuff, because the bathroom looked like a total gym. I mean, these girls looked *really*

My pink dress

happy to be going to this party. I tried to join in the fun by doing some sort of gymnastics move, but the best I could do was a headstand with my feet leaning against the wall. Pretty lame, huh?

"Did you hear?" a girl named Olivia announced in between brushing her teeth. "They invited the boys' team, too!"

All the girls squealed when they heard that. "Really? Are you sure?" they screamed.

"Helena, is it true? Did your dad invite the boys, too?" asked a girl named Selina.

"I don't know," said Helena, who was by a mirror twisting her hair into some incredibly complicated bun. She was a little taller than most of the girls and absolutely beautiful. "My dad hasn't said a word. He loves to surprise me."

Just then, Sophia came cartwheeling through the bathroom doorway, landing with her arms outstretched.

"Guess what?" she announced, strutting around a bit. "I know something you guys don't. I just talked to Costas and…"

"The boys' team is coming, too!" cried Selina.

"I knew it!" shouted Olivia. Sophia looked majorly ticked off that everybody already knew her big secret.

"Okay, who wants to do my hair?" asked Olivia.

The next hour was really fun. Everybody took turns doing each other's hair—Alexis did mine long and straight, with French braids in back. I brushed out her pigtails and put some glitter in her bangs, which made her look really cute. Then we all got dressed. I didn't want to ruin my look, but I also couldn't leave my backpack with the angel stuff in it. So I slipped it on and met everybody down in the lobby.

"You all look beautiful, girls," said Coach Gretel. She was dressed up, too, in flowing white pants, a pretty shirt, and big earrings. She hustled us onto the shuttle bus, and we headed for the pier.

I couldn't believe how awesomely huge the yacht was when we got there. It was the kind you see in movies. You know, the movies about really, really rich people. We boarded up a ramp that took us into a red-carpeted room with carved wood walls and a chandelier. Can you imagine all of this on a boat?

At the top of the ramp, Paolo shook my hand. "Welcome, Hannah!" he said. "You're very good with secrets!" he added, winking.

Then Captain X walked over to us. "Just a little treat for each of you," he said grandly. "The photos that we shot this morning at practice!" He handed me a framed photo, too.

My photo

"But how did you get this photo of me?" I asked. My photo hadn't been taken at the gym. It was a glossy shot of me sitting on the steps of the Parthenon with Catastrophe in my lap. I had no idea that my picture was being taken! I didn't like it one bit. I felt like someone had spied on me.

"We didn't want to leave you out, Hannah," Captain X said with a big smile. "You'll have to ask Paolo how he got this wonderful photo."

I turned back to Paolo. Had the sneak been carrying a camera all day? If he had been, I sure hadn't seen it. Maybe he had snapped the picture before we even met today. I thought that would be totally creepy. I was going to ask him when he had taken the picture, but he was busy welcoming the team. So I dropped the subject.

"Let's see your picture, Alexis," I said. She held it out. "Wow, that's fantastic!" In the photo, Alexis looked beautiful as she performed a split with her arms stretched over her head.

"I *do* look pretty good, don't I?" asked Alexis.

"You look like a real winner," I said. Even though Captain X's picture was so nice, I decided that I would still give Alexis the picture I had taken of her in the gym, too. I figured that I should add some neat things to it first, to make it stand out on its own.

We were shown to rooms where we could change into our swimsuits and leave our belongings, if we wanted. Alexis and I shared a cabin. It was decorated in deep-purple velvet, with big, soft furniture. NUMBER 7—our room number—was carved right into the door.

Soon the ship set sail. Once Alexis and I put on our swimsuits, we were escorted to the deck. I couldn't believe there was actually a swimming pool built into the yacht! And it was totally packed with kids having a great time. There was also a ton of food, which I immediately sampled. I tried *dolmades*, which are stuffed grape leaves; *spanakopita*, which is a spinach-cheese pie; and *baklava*, which is a sticky, flaky sweet. They all tasted so good! This definitely had all the makings of a perfect evening—a live band was playing Greek music, the stars shone in the pale pink sky, and over by the railing, boys and girls were flirting with each other.

I shot a few pictures with my camera. Then I decided that nobody would notice if I went exploring. So I ducked back into the cabin and examined one room after another. I guess you could call me snoopy, but I figured this would be my only chance to explore a private yacht! I just knew it would be full of interesting stuff.

First, I found the library. Every single book was in Greek. I thought *that* was interesting—I had never seen so many Greek books before in my life. Then I found the bathroom, which had gold swans for faucets and the biggest Jacuzzi tub I'd ever seen. That was definitely interesting, too.

But the next interesting thing I found nearly scared me half to death...

Chapter 11

A Greek Tragedy?

Carved into each door I came to was a scene or characters from Greek mythology. I was careful to knock on each door before I entered—I knocked on Zeus' nose and Apollo's chariot. They both were locked. Then I came to a door carved with two ancient Greek theater masks. There was a happy mask, which stood for comedy, and a sad mask, which stood for tragedy. I was hoped the tragic mask wasn't some kind of bad omen for me.

The unlocked door

Nobody answered my knock. So I turned the knob and found the door was unlocked. I slowly opened it and peeked inside a tiny room crammed with all different types of treasures: navigation maps, a brass compass, a bunch of electrical equipment, and radio instruments. There was a bunk bed, a desk, a map of Italy, and some family photos on the walls. I snuck in and immediately checked out the books first. They were in English, Greek, and another language that looked a little like French.

Then, on the desk, I found the little black book that Paolo had written in. *So this is Paolo's cabin!* I thought.

My heart started beating really fast. I just had to see what kind of stuff he wrote in that little black book. But what if I got caught? I tiptoed back to the door and listened. I heard waves rippling against the side of the ship and faint sounds of the party up on deck. I didn't hear anyone moving around where I was. I figured the coast was clear.

I slowly crept back to the desk and opened the book. It was written in the same three languages as the library books. It looked like a daily log. There was a date at the top of each page. Every day, the ship's position and the weather were noted in English. On the right-hand side was a lot of writing, kind of like a diary.

I flipped through the book until I got to the party page. There was my name—Hannah Martin—just as Paolo had said, at the bottom of the guest list. There was lots more writing on the two pages before and on the page after. But it wasn't written in English. I did see "Martin" once or twice, though. How could I figure out what he was saying about me? I didn't want to just take the black book, because that would be wrong.

Me, spying

Besides, Paolo would certainly notice it was gone. I'd probably get in major trouble— and maybe Alexis would, too—if that happened.

I thought for a moment. Suddenly, an idea came to me. I pulled out my angel camera and took a photo of the pages dated today and yesterday. I had to wait for one picture to print before I could shoot the next. While I waited between shots, I crept over to the door to listen. I couldn't hear a thing. But after I'd shot four pages of the book, I heard footsteps.

My heart leapt into my throat. I got the feeling that my little investigation might turn into a full-fledged tragedy at any minute.

I dashed over to the desk and shut the little black book. I shoved the camera and the photos into the outside pocket of my backpack. Again, I heard the footsteps.

What should I do?

Chapter 12

Balance Is Everything

I decided to slip out the door before anyone found me. But I didn't get very far. After I had taken about three steps down the hall, who was standing right in front of me but...*Paolo!*

"Are you lost, Hannah?" he asked. He didn't seem the least bit upset.

"Ummm, I guess I am...," I stammered.

Paolo walked past me into his quarters, picked up the black book, and tucked it into his pocket. Then he came back and held out his arm for me to link my hand around.

"This way, my little American friend," he said, leading me back up to the party. He was being so sweet, chatting with me all the way, that I felt really guilty.

If he only knew what I've just done! I thought. If

anyone ever snuck into my room and read my journal, I'd probably never forgive them. There aren't too many things that are unforgivable in this world, but, for me, that's certainly one of them.

"Where have you been, Hannah?" asked Alexis as we arrived at the pool. She was dripping wet.

"She was wandering around down below and got lost," said Paolo. He unlinked my arm from his now that I was safe and sound. "I rescued her," he said.

I shrugged, like I was a helpless little girl. Captain X came up to me and Alexis.

"You promised you would learn to dance *syrtaki*," he said to me. "Don't you think we should make Hannah keep her promise, Alexis?"

Alexis smiled, grabbing ahold of my hand. "Absolutely!" she exclaimed. "Come on, Hannah, I'll teach you!"

Syrtaki with Paolo

As Alexis whisked me onto the dance floor, I noticed musicians playing instruments I'd never seen before. The music was totally different from anything I've ever heard. I really liked it. It had a nice, festive feeling. Alexis and Helena showed me *syrtaki*, and other dancers joined us on the dance floor.

"Balance is everything, my *schnitzel*," Alexis told me, just the way Coach Gretel would say.

"Imagine you're empty inside, *schotzie*," instructed Helena, tapping my tummy with a Coach Gretel–like gesture. "Just full of air and space." Both the girls started giggling over the Gretel impersonations. Even Coach Gretel herself was laughing. She joined us in the dancing, too.

I practiced with Alexis, Helena, and Coach Gretel for a few minutes. Once I had most of the moves down, I danced with some of the guys from the boys' team. Then I found myself dancing with Paolo. I would have been a lot more nervous dancing with Paolo if I hadn't seen something that totally distracted me. Out of the corner of my eye, I noticed that Sophia was whispering to Costas and pointing at Alexis. It looked pretty suspicious to me. I didn't like it at all.

Suddenly, everyone started another dance with a Greek name so long, I couldn't pronounce it. Helena was waving a red scarf, and everyone started dancing behind her so they looked like a big snake. I decided that learning two Greek dances in one night was too much for me. So I thanked Paolo and slipped away to fix up the photo I had taken of Alexis at the gym.

"I'm changing back into my dress," I told her as I left the dance floor. "Keep an eye on Sophia, huh?"

"Okay," she said.

I headed for the cabin that Alexis and I shared. When I got inside, I pulled out my scissors and glue and some silver glitter that I'd saved from Paolo's invitations. I cut out two wings and pasted the silver glitter all over them. Then I took out the photo of Alexis I'd taken that morning. I stuck the glittery wings on it.

"Alexis, you look like an angel!" I said out loud. "You'll fly all the way to the Olympics!"

"Very good," said a voice.

I would have jumped out of my skin, except I recognized the voice instantly. It belonged to Demetriel, my guardian angel.

"Hi, Demi!" I said.

"The wings are wonderful, Hannah," she said. "Although they should be attached a little higher, like real angels' wings."

Alexis with angel wings

"Thanks for pointing that out, Demi," I said. I adjusted the wings while the glue was still wet.

"Much better!" she replied. "That will help inspire Alexis to keep her courage and never give up."

"You really think it will help?" I asked.

"Most definitely," said Demi. "Now, about these horrible notes, Hannah…"

"Can you tell me who's sending them?" I asked.

"Of course not. That's your job to find out," said Demi. "But I *can* tell you that this person could be very dangerous, so you must be careful."

"I'm in danger?" I asked.

"No, not you, Hannah," Demi assured me. "But Alexis is. Do not let her out of your sight, Hannah."

"But she's out of my sight right now," I said.

"You must return to her as soon as you can," Demi instructed. "There's one more thing—you will be playing a game tonight. But no matter what happens, Hannah, you must remember that it's only a game."

"Okay," I said. A game didn't sound all that important.

"What's happening with Alexis is no game, though," Demi added. "It's very serious."

"I'll remember that," I assured Demi. "Now I better go find Alexis, right?"

But there was no answer. Demi had left without warning, as usual. As I propped Alexis's photo up on the table to arrange the wings, there was a sudden loud knock on the door.

Chapter 13

Killer

"It's me, Hannah!" Alexis called as she walked in. She saw her photo right away. "Oh, I love it!" she burst out in excitement. "You made me look like an angel!"

"Exactly!" I said. "Your *wings* haven't melted and your *head* is attached, all safe and sound."

Alexis's smile grew even bigger as she understood my meaning. "And those notes are just plain stupid!" she replied. "Whenever I get bothered by them, I'll look at me and my wings...and fly!"

"Yes!" I said enthusiastically. Demi was totally right. This was definitely a boost for Alexis.

"Hannah," said Alexis. "I came in to tell you about something that might be suspicious. I noticed Maria whispering with Costas. She was pointing at me the whole time. Then, as soon as she saw me looking at her, she turned away like she was caught or something."

"I saw Sophia doing that, too. But I'm not sure that it means anything," I said.

"But listen to this," continued Alexis. "Maria walked over to Sophia and then they both did the same thing—whispering and pointing right at me."

"Maybe they're planning to play another trick on you," I said.

"I just hope they're not planning something worse," Alexis replied.

"What do you mean?" I asked.

"Well, think about it, Hannah," Alexis replied. "I'm the youngest of the gymnasts, and I might be good enough to make the Olympic team."

"So?" I asked.

"So, like you said before, maybe they're jealous."

"Maybe," I agreed. I opened my journal, checking my suspect list and notes.

"I hate to say this, but I've thought it over a lot. I wouldn't be surprised if Sophia and Maria are writing those notes," said Alexis.

"Or maybe someone they know is writing the notes for them," I said. I wasn't sure about any of this—I was just thinking out loud.

"Like who?" asked Alexis. "Costas?"

I'd been most suspicious of Paolo so far. But

now I decided to focus on Sophia, Maria, and Costas.

"Let's keep an eye on the three of them tonight," I said. "But remember, Alexis, your main job is to concentrate on your Olympic goal."

"I know," Alexis agreed. "But I want to help you spy, too—it's kind of fun."

"Okay," I said. "Just don't lose your wings in the meantime."

Alexis giggled and flapped her arms like they were angel wings as we headed back to the deck. Everybody was in a circle, gathered around Sophia.

"We're going to play a little game tonight," Sophia was saying.

Well, you know me, I'm always up for games, so Alexis and I quickly joined the group. Sophia ripped sheets of white paper into little squares. Then she held up one square for us all to see. It had a picture of an eye on it, with little lashes stuck around the rim.

"The game is called Killer," she explained. Well, I definitely didn't like the sound of that! I exchanged a look with Alexis, who didn't look happy, either.

"I know this game!" cried Maria.

"I kind of hate that game," said Helena. "It's too creepy!"

"How do you play?" asked Christos, a friend of Costas's.

Sophia got a Queen-of-the-Universe look on her face and slowly gazed around the group. I could tell that she was trying to intimidate us.

"It *is* a creepy game," she said with a little smile. "That's what makes it so fun. We all need to relax after our hard work, right?"

"Right," Costas agreed. (He would probably agree to anything Sophia said.) "How do you play?" he asked.

"We all pick a piece of paper," Sophia began. "Everyone's paper will be blank, except for one." She stared slowly and dramatically at each of us again.

"Okay, get on with it," said Christos, rolling his eyes.

"One person will get this eye," she said, holding up the eyeball picture again. "And that person is the *killer*."

Sophia's killer eye.

"So what's that supposed to mean?" I asked, irritated.

"It means that all night long, the killer tries to make eye contact with the rest of us. And when the killer catches your eye, he winks."

"And that means you're dead!" shouted Maria gleefully.

"Once you're dead, you can look people in the eye again. But you can't wink, not unless you're the killer. Whoever is still alive by nine o'clock wins!"

"What a dumb game," said Alexis. But I could

see it made her a little nervous, considering the threats she had received.

"Come on, Alexis. Be a good sport and play with us," Costas said, pouting a little.

"But I thought we were going to eat and dance and swim tonight," I said.

"We are!" said Sophia. "That's what great about this game. You can play it while you're doing other things."

"What do the winners get?" asked Helena.

"Uhhh...nothing...," said Sophia.

"How about we put a crown of olive leaves on their heads?" suggested one of the boys, laughing.

"That's pretty good. Just like they used to do in the ancient Olympics!" said Helena.

"The winners get nothing," Sophia repeated. "They just get to win."

I was watching Sophia very closely. My brain started to work overtime. *Is there a reason why we're playing a game where you don't want to look at anyone? Would that give Sophia a chance to slip out and leave Alexis a note without anyone noticing?*

"So is everybody in?" asked Sophia, tossing her braids.

I decided if everybody was going around not looking at each other, it would give me a chance to spy. And since no one else spoke up to object, I kept quiet, too. Sophia stretched out her arms dramatically.

"Let the games begin!" she announced, just like they do at the opening of the Olympics.

"Costas, let me borrow your cap," she said. She tossed the folded scraps of paper inside and passed the hat to Alexis. *Why Alexis first?* I wondered. *Does that mean something?*

Alexis reached in and pulled out a piece of paper. She opened it all secretively, but I managed to see a relieved look on her face. The piece of paper was probably blank. Then the hat was passed around and everyone else took a piece of paper. I walked over to the corner to open mine. Blank. Thank goodness. I'd play the game, but I sure didn't want to be the killer. I'd be too busy winking at everybody to have any time to spy. I glanced up. Everybody's eyes were turned down.

"Where do we go now?" asked Olivia. I didn't look at her, but I figured she wasn't looking at me, either. A couple of the girls started giggling nervously.

"This is pretty weird, not looking at anybody," said Selina.

"It is, isn't it?" Christos agreed.

"We're just about to sail past Mr. Xenos's island!" Paolo announced. (He and the other adults weren't playing our dumb game.) "If you look out the starboard side, you'll see it."

We all followed each other's feet to the right side of the ship to look. I saw a few houses scattered here and there on the island.

"Does Mr. Xenos own the houses on that island, too?" I asked the feet next to me. They belonged to some boy I didn't know.

"Are you kidding?" he answered back. "Mr. Xenos owns every stone! He's practically the Greek god of that island!"

Captain X,
the Greek god.

Chapter 14

Only a Game

"Lemonade, anyone?" called Paolo from the other side of the pool. He was squeezing fresh lemonade and passing it out to whoever wanted some. Most of us shuffled back over his way. I didn't care much about the game, so I watched all the kids watching each other's feet.

"Gather round, winners!" said Captain X.

"Winners?" Helena asked.

"Yes! Let's have a toast!" her dad shouted. He waited until everyone had a glass of lemonade and then raised his high. We all raised our glasses as well.

"To the fine athletes of Greece!" he said. "Whether you end up on the Olympic team or not, every one of you is a winner!"

Yasou!

"*Ya sou!*" everybody shouted, smiling. (It rhymed with "yahoo.")

"*Ya sou!*" I repeated. I figured that it probably meant "Cheers!"

We drank our lemonade, and then most of the kids went swimming. I decided to keep my eye on the people on my list, especially Sophia and Maria. Alexis took a dive into the pool. Somehow, she muffed it and belly-flopped, splashing everybody.

"What's the matter with Alexis?" I heard Maria ask, sounding really concerned. Alexis surfaced right next to me.

A belly flop?

"Haven't you noticed?" asked Sophia. "Alexis hasn't been focused since she arrived at pre-trials. She's losing it."

"How can you say that?" Alexis burst out. I could tell that she was very embarrassed. As she swam toward the ladder, I thought she might be crying. I couldn't really tell, though, with all the water on her face.

"But it *does* seem like something's been wrong lately, Alexis," Helena gently added as Alexis got out of the pool. "Do you think you might be sick or something?"

Well, did that do it. Alexis *totally* lost her temper. "Nothing is wrong with me!" she screamed at the top of her lungs. "So I lost my balance *one* time. So what?" she hollered, and sat down with her arms crossed.

I quickly went over to her. Just then, out of the corner of my eye, I saw Sophia and Costas wander away from the pool along the side of the ship. I dropped my towel in Alexis's lap.

"I'm sorry to leave you, Alexis, but I'm going to follow those two," I whispered. "Keep an eye on Maria, will you?" Alexis managed a nod, then wiped her face with the towel.

I crept along the ship's side, following Sophia and Costas at a distance. They strolled up toward the bow, which is the front of the ship. Suddenly, Costas glanced over his shoulder right at me! I quickly pretended to be gazing out at Captain X's island as we continued to circle it. I stood there, not daring to turn around, and watched the moon's reflection rippling up and down in the water.

"Please take care of Alexis," I whispered into the moonlight, hoping my angels would hear me. "And help me find out who's trying to push her over the edge."

"I hear that you spy on people," sneered a voice behind me. "I also hear you talk to *angels*."

Shivers ran up and down my spine. I could tell from the gritty rasp of the voice that it was Sophia. I turned around slowly and gave her the cold glare that I reserve for the Fudge.

"Hello, Sophia," I remarked.

"Well, is it true?" she pressed. "I just heard you talking into thin air, Hannah. So where are these angels I've heard about?"

"If you must know, I was talking to myself," I said. I started to walk back toward the pool. But Sophia stepped right into my path, facing me square on. I felt like I was back in my Geneva kickball game, and she was definitely a worthy opponent.

"In Greece, we have a name for people who talk to themselves," she said snottily. "We call them lunatics."

I laughed, but it came out like an uncomfortable choke. "We use the same word in English," I said, casually trying to sidestep her. No chance—she was solidly planted right in front of me, determined not to let me go.

"'Lunatic' means "'touched by the moon,'" she said intensely. "Crazy, out of control."

I hated the look in her eyes. I felt like she despised me.

"Are you dead yet?" she asked with a thin smile.

I knew she was talking about the game. "Nope," I answered, still casually trying to pass her. "I'm very much alive."

She cocked her head close to my face, trying to catch my glance. But I stared at the ground. "Maybe it's your turn to die now," she whispered.

Well, that did it. I wasn't going to let her stand there and torment me like I was some kind of voodoo doll. "What do you want from me, Sophia?" I burst out, looking her straight in the eyes. "You act like you have something against me, and I want to know why!" I demanded.

Sophia took a moment to gather herself. I had totally caught her off guard. "Because you're poisoning our team," she said slowly.

"What? What are you talking about?"

"Don't try to act innocent. Ever since you showed up, Alexis has been gradually losing her edge. She's preoccupied, she's not a team player—she's off balance."

I was confused. The threats had started before I even arrived in Greece.

"You're blaming *me* for Alexis's behavior?" I said, shocked.

"Who else could be to blame?" Sophia asked, smirking. "Everything was going well. We had a great team. In fact, we're the *first* womens' gymnastics team Greece has ever had. And Alexis is one of our best—if not *the* best." Sophia slapped her hand on the ship's rail for emphasis. "Then, suddenly, some girl who talks to angels shows up out of nowhere, and our best athlete starts falling apart. What do you expect me to think?"

"I suppose it could look like that," I mused. "But it's far from the truth."

The moonlight struck Sophia's face. Her eyes

were cold as ice. I couldn't read what she was thinking. Was she just trying to use me as a scapegoat? Or was she really concerned about her teammate?

Sophia's moonlit eyes stared into mine, and suddenly she winked. "You're dead," she said with a crooked little smile as she turned on her heels and took off toward the pool.

Chapter 15

Worry Beads

Talk about a stressful night! After my confrontation with Sophia, I couldn't wait to get off Captain X's yacht. Here I had thought it would be the perfect evening, when really all I had to show for it was being winked to death. Finally (and not a moment too soon), it was time to head back for the mainland. Alexis and I went to our cabin to change into our clothes.

Moonlight poured through the porthole. Suddenly, Alexis grabbed my arm hard and pressed her palm over her mouth. She was shaking like a bird. I looked down. Bits of torn paper were scattered on the floor, where they glittered in the moonlight. When I realized what they were, I screamed. I was immediately sorry that I had. If the

Moonlight through the porthole

85

creep who did this was watching, I didn't want him to know that he had scared me.

"Your wings," I whispered. "The wings I pasted onto your picture." But what I didn't say was, *The wings Demi knew would encourage you to keep going.*

"Somebody broke in here while we were gone!" gasped Alexis, terror in her eyes. "They ripped my wings to pieces!"

I eyeballed the cabin to be sure nobody was still lurking in it. This was definitely not a good situation. First of all, someone had trespassed in our room while we were gone. (Whoops, I guess I kind of just did that, too.) Second, this was another threat. Third, and maybe worst of all, we had been completely wrong about who had been terrorizing Alexis.

"We were with Sophia, Maria, and Costas all night long," I said.

"So it's not them!" cried Alexis. She dropped into a purple chair. "If it's not them, then who's doing this to me?"

"Whoever it is, they're obviously here on this ship," I said.

"And they weren't with the rest of us tonight," added Alexis.

"Or they snuck out for just a few minutes," I said.

"Everything is so wrong," cried Alexis, tears welling in her eyes.

"We'll get to the bottom of this," I said, determined. "You'll make it through the tryouts, you'll do great. And then you'll go on to the Olympics, and the whole world will see you win."

As I talked, Alexis shook her head miserably.

"No, Hannah, no," she sobbed. "It's over. I'm too scared to do this anymore."

I knew I had to think of something, and fast. I had to convince Alexis to go on.

"But, Alexis—" I began.

"Stop it!" she said, interrupting me. "Listen, Hannah! It's over. I'm off the team—I quit!"

"You don't mean that, Alexis," I said. "You *can* do this. You *can* go on in spite of these threats."

Alexis giving up

"No, I can't," she said.

"I can't" is probably the worst possible thing an athlete can say. In fact, it's the worst thing anybody can say, because it usually means failure is right around the corner.

All of a sudden, Alexis lost it. Tears poured out like a rainstorm. She slid onto the floor, sobbing, her head in her hands. I quickly sat down beside her.

"Alexis, don't let this get to you," I said. But at the same time, I wondered how she could *not* let this get to her. I mean, here she was in danger of losing everything she'd worked her whole life for! And maybe she was in even more danger than that. What if her life was actually being threatened?

"I've tried everything," she sobbed. "I've tried not to think about it. I've tried to pretend it's not important. I've tried to focus on the tryouts…"

"And you've been doing great!" I assured her.

"But this is too much!" she cried. She picked up a few silvery bits of wing and threw them into the air for emphasis. "I can't do it anymore!"

Just then, we heard Paolo's voice. "Party's over!" he was saying. The yacht had pulled into the pier, so Alexis and I gathered ourselves, walked out of the cabin, and thanked Captain X and his crew, even though our hearts were dragging.

On the shuttle bus home, I pulled out my worry beads and started flipping them over and over in my fingers. Alexis just sat there, weeping silently into her hands. Her tears overflowed and started dripping onto the floor. As I watched Alexis, I realized my worry beads weren't working—I was more worried than ever. Tomorrow was the final practice before the actual Olympic tryouts began. How was I going to help Alexis in time?

Chapter 16

Missing Piece?

I was up early the next morning standing on the balcony. Sophia and Maria had already left to meet Costas and Christos. As I walked in the room, I noticed a piece of paper under the door to the hall. I immediately got an uneasy feeling.

I crept over and bent down to pick it up. Sure enough, the piece of paper looked just like the other nasty notes—black ink on white paper. I slipped back out onto the balcony with it, because there was no way I was going to let Alexis see it.

But, of course, it was in Greek—so I couldn't read it!

"Lorielle," I whispered, "if I'm supposed to read this, please help me translate it. *Please.*"

I stared at the page. Seconds later, the writing turned into angel code! It began:

☆ ☺ ☆ ☺ = ☆ ♡ ◉ △

In English, it read:

> EMERGENCY! MEET ME AT 2:00 AT THE
> AMPHITHEATER. IF YOU DON'T, YOU'LL BE
> SORRY. YOU KNOW WHAT HAPPENED TO
> MEDUSA'S VICTIMS—WHEN THEIR EYES
> MET HERS, THEY TURNED TO STONE.

Before I even had time to think, Alexis sat up in bed. I quickly stashed the note in my backpack.

"I'm late for practice," she said apathetically.

"But practice doesn't start until ten today, remember?" I said.

"Oh," she answered. I didn't hear one ounce of enthusiasm in her voice. It sounded to me like she'd already given up the fight. It was like she decided to go to practice because she thought she had to—not because she wanted to.

"Any more death threats?" she asked.

"No," I lied. I knew it was important to protect her from this new one. "But I did remember something that I forgot to tell you about last night!"

I dug into my backpack and pulled out the photos I'd taken on the ship. I also pulled out the notes about Nike's head and Icarus' wings.

"These are pages from Paolo's little black

book. But since I don't know the Greek alphabet, I can't compare the handwriting," I explained.

Alexis picked up the notes and set them on her bed next to the photos. Slowly, she looked back and forth between the two piles.

"Can you tell if the same person wrote all of these?" I asked.

But Alexis didn't say a word. She was too engrossed in the materials before her. After a few moments, she paused and clasped her hands together. Then she looked at me, her eyes wide.

"The same person wrote both of these. It's identical handwriting."

"Are you sure?" I asked.

"Absolutely positive," she said.

"You're really, really, *really* sure?" I asked.

"Look, Hannah," Alexis pointed out. "The word 'wings' is misspelled in this diary *and* in the Icarus note. A Greek person wouldn't make that same spelling error twice."

"But this is Paolo's diary," I said. "Isn't Paolo Greek?"

"No," said Alexis. "Paolo is Italian."

"I didn't know that!" I said. "So *that's* the other language in his diary—Italian!"

"Exactly," said Alexis.

"So Paolo's our culprit," I said. "That creep!"

"But why would Paolo want me out of the trials?" asked Alexis as she paced the floor.

"Oh my gosh, Alexis!" I cried. "I bet it's because his boss, Mr. Xenos, wants Helena to be on the Olympic team, and he thinks you're too much competition for her!"

"If that's true, then this is even worse than I thought," said Alexis. "Mr. Xenos is a very powerful man. If he wants me out of the Olympics, I bet he can keep me out."

"Do you think Helena knows about this?" I asked.

Alexis began to look pretty angry. "I don't know—maybe all three of them planned this. Maybe Helena is the one sneaking the notes to me. And maybe Mr. Xenos is trying to cover it up by throwing the party on his yacht."

"This is beginning to make some sense, Alexis."

"But what should I do?" she asked.

"You should just continue to be the awesome gymnast that you are. Isn't today the final practice before tryouts?" I asked.

"Yes. Anybody who doesn't show up today can't compete in the Olympic trials," she said as she began to do her stretching.

Alexis on the bar

"All you have to do is show up for practice. You got that, Alexis? Just show up," I said. "Leave the rest to me."

Chapter 17

Switcheroo

I went to work the minute Alexis left. A lot of things were becoming clear to me now. But some things still didn't make sense.

First of all, we knew Paolo was sending the notes. But unless Helena helped, how did he sneak into the gym and the dorm? Come to think of it, where had he been when the fishnet fell on me and Alexis? He had definitely been spying on me—taking pictures, finding out my name, showing up to take me shopping—all to figure out how to get to Alexis.

Second, was Captain X instructing Paolo? It was obvious that Captain X adored Helena. She was his only daughter, and he would do anything for her. He had even named his yacht *Helena*. I remembered how he'd been interrogating me at the Plaka café that night, too. He was probably gathering information for his little "Project: Scare Alexis."

Third, this morning's note told Alexis to meet at two o'clock—right in the middle of the final practice. That way, if she fell for it and missed practice, Coach Gretel would have no choice but to eliminate her from the Olympic trials. Very clever.

It seemed like these guys knew exactly what they were doing. But they had no idea they were dealing with Hannah Martin and her angels.

"Let's go, angels!" I said. I quickly combed my hair into pigtails, looping them up so they were nice and short. Then I tried to squeeze into one of Alexis's gym suits. Not a chance! She's so tiny.

Let's go, angels !

"Sophia won't mind if I borrow hers, will she, angels?" I asked. I figured Demi would give me her usual tug on the hair if she objected. But no tug, so I slipped on Sophia's blue-and-white Greek team uniform.

I checked the mirror. Not bad—I could easily pass for Alexis at a distance (as long as I didn't have to do a backflip). By one-thirty, I was on my way to the amphitheater to make an unexpected visit.

Chapter 18

Adio!

When I arrived at the amphitheater, I circled around the top row of seats, checking to be sure there wasn't some kind of trap set for Alexis. There didn't seem to be any. In fact, the place was completely empty—not even a tourist in sight.

I walked toward the stage. The minute I sat down, my furry buddy came bounding down the steps toward me.

"Catastrophe!" I said. "You seem to show up wherever I am." He jumped into my lap, curling up into a little ball. He stared up at me with his green eyes while I petted him.

"Well, Alexis," said Paolo's voice suddenly behind me. "I'm sorry you had to miss your final practice."

I just sat there looking at the ground, not moving. Paolo walked a few steps down until he was right in front of me. I slowly lifted my head up until his eyes met mine. His face twisted in shock when he realized it was me.

"Hannah!" he exclaimed. He tried to act natural, but it was too late.

"Hello, Paolo," I said. "Are you disappointed it's me? If you're looking for Alexis, she's at practice with the rest of the girls."

Paolo just stood there looking awfully perplexed.

"I'm sure you *are* disappointed, Paolo," I continued. "After all, now Alexis will be trying out for the Olympic team, and she'll probably get picked! It looks like your little plan isn't going to work, huh?"

He shook his head, trying to understand that he'd been defeated. He looked at me in total disbelief. Then he sat down beside me. Catastrophe bared his teeth and hissed at him.

"Good little tiger!" I whispered, stroking the cat's fur.

"Maybe you can straighten something out for me, Ms. Martin," Paolo said.

"Yes, I probably can," I said victoriously.

"Where exactly did you come from? And what made you decide to meddle in Alexis's business?"

"Meddle?" I asked. "You call it meddling?"

"Well, isn't it?" he said. "You became her little helper—her bodyguard."

"If it hadn't been for me, you just might have

knocked Alexis out of competition, right?" I asked back.

"Yes," he said bitterly. "But everywhere I went, *you* were there. In the Plàka—shopping. Sneaking around in my cabin. And today, here you are again. It's like you show up out of nowhere."

"You and Mr. Xenos really thought you could force a place for Helena on the team by hurting another athlete, didn't you? Don't you know how cruel that is?" I asked.

"Mr. Xenos?" said Paolo, looking confused.

"Yes. And was Helena in on this, too?" I asked. "Was she the one delivering all the notes?"

"Nobody knew about this but me," said Paolo. "I didn't need anybody to deliver the notes. I just told the guards I was delivering important notes from Mr. Xenos, and they let me right through."

"So Helena had no idea?" I asked.

"No, *oji!*" Paolo said emphatically. "And if Mr. Xenos ever finds out what I've done, I will most definitely be fired!"

Suddenly, a car screeched up on the road behind us, and a familiar voice boomed across the open theater. "Paolo!" it bellowed. "Don't move!"

I spun around to see three people jumping out of a limousine: Captain X, Coach Gretel, and Alexis!

Paolo panicked. He leapt to his feet and took off like a shot. He raced across the seats down

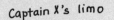

Captain X's limo

toward the amphitheater's stage. But he didn't get far, because Catastrophe was faster. That little guy flew into the air and landed at Paolo's feet. Paolo tripped over the cat and crashed onto the stage. Then he just lay there, like a character in some ancient Greek play who had been tragically defeated.

Of course, Alexis and Coach Gretel were at the stage in a flash, leaping from seat to seat like lightning. Even Captain X was surprisingly fast.

TRAGIC PAOLO

"I know everything, Paolo!" he roared, loping down toward the stage. He went into a whole explosion of Greek words, and, for once, I was glad that I couldn't understand what he was saying.

"What were you thinking?" he concluded in English.

"I did it for Helena," Paolo answered, hanging his head in embarrassment "And for you, Xenos. I was sure you'd appreciate it if I got Helena on the team!"

"Of course I want Helena to win!" said Captain X. "But not by torturing poor Alexis! Every girl has to win on her own merit!"

"I didn't intend to really hurt Alexis," Paolo

continued. "I only wanted to throw her off balance."

"Which is *exactly* what you did!" Coach Gretel scolded, putting her arm around Alexis. "How dare you! When Alexis told me this morning what was going on, I didn't waste a moment contacting your boss."

"And I'm very glad you got to me in time," said Mr. Xenos.

"So I suppose I won't be promoted to first mate now, will I?" Paolo moaned as he got to his feet.

"Aha! So that's what this is all about," said Captain X, shaking his head. "My poor misguided Paolo—shame on you."

I felt a little ashamed myself. Here I'd been suspecting all those people, who turned out to be totally innocent. I exchanged a look with Alexis. I could see she was feeling the same way.

I heard a siren in the distance. I turned around to see if an ambulance had driven up by Captain X's limo. But, of course, there was nothing there. I realized that I was the only one hearing the siren. As everybody continued to sort things out, I quickly pulled Alexis aside.

"Alexis, it's time for me to go home now," I whispered.

"What? But…why?" she asked, looking disappointed.

"Because now I know that everything with

you will be just fine," I said with a smile.

"But can't you stay for the tryouts?" she asked.

"I wish I could, but I'm afraid not," I answered. "I know you'll do great, though!"

"Thank you, Hannah," said Alexis, giving me a big hug. "I'm so lucky you came to Greece! Watch for me at the Olympics, okay?"

"You bet I will."

I picked up Catastrophe as Alexis walked back to Coach Gretel.

"I'm gonna miss you, buddy," I said. "I sure do wish you could come home with me."

The little cat looked into my eyes sadly, as if he knew exactly what I was saying. Then he licked my fingers with his tiny pink tongue.

Adio, Catastrophe!

"*Adio*, Catastrophe!" I whispered. He blinked, and then I was gone.

Chapter 19

A Cat and a Hat

Ms. Montgomery's big green eyes were looking into mine. She was saying something to me, but I could barely make it out.

"You'd better sit on the bench for a while," I think she was telling me.

"Um…okay," I agreed. If there was one thing I could definitely use, it was a break. So I happily turned to head toward the bench when Ms. Montgomery grabbed my arm.

"What's going on here?" she asked me sternly.

"What do you mean?" I asked.

She slowly looked me up and down. "The hat?" she finally said, pointing at my head. "And the cat?" she said, pointing to my arms.

I looked down in my arms, and there curled into a ball was little Catastrophe! I guess I must have been so flustered by being whisked back from my angel trip that I totally didn't notice him all snuggled up. I stuck my nose into his fur.

"I can't believe you made it home with me, little buddy," I whispered.

"So what's with the cat and the hat?" Ms. Montgomery asked. "I didn't see them here a minute ago."

"Well...I don't really know," I said, backing off the field. "Guess I should get to the bench, huh?" I said, spinning around on my heels and high-tailing it across the field. I had no idea what to say, so I just hoped that Ms. Montgomery would forget all about it after the game.

I sat down on the bench with a bunch of my teammates and pulled off my hat. It was the fisherman's cap. *Thanks for the souvenirs, angels!* I thought.

"Hey, where'd the cat come from?" hollered Jimmy Fudge. I guess he was out of the game for a while, too. He came over to pat Catastrophe on the head. Surprisingly, Catastrophe didn't hiss at him.

"You're a good kitty, aren't you?" said the Fudge in a high-pitched voice, the kind you use when talking to babies. "Don't you have a home?" he asked. "Hey, Martin. This cat doesn't have a collar. He must need a home." *Oh, great!* I thought. That's all I needed—for the Fudge to take Catastrophe home. Then I'd have to visit him all the time.

"I'm adopting him," I quickly said.

"You are?" my parents both said at once. Whoops, I guess they overheard me. I didn't realize they were sitting right behind me on the bleachers.

"Ummm, well...I've seen this cat before, and we've become buddies, and...oh, *pleeease?*" I begged my mom. She immediately looked at me with her "no way" expression. But my dad smiled at me and gave me the thumbs-up.

"Hey, if you adopt him, can I visit sometimes?" asked the Fudge. He was petting Catastrophe under the chin, talking baby-kitty talk to him.

"Well, I..." I had no idea what to say. The Fudge visiting Catastrophe—at *my* house? Yuck! But the more I looked at him petting Catastrophe, the more he actually looked...human. Maybe he did have an ounce of kindness hidden inside him after all.

The Fudge has a good side?

I looked down at Catastrophe. If I was nice to the Fudge, maybe my angels would help me convince my mom to keep the cat. "Sure, you can visit him," I told him. Then I turned to my mom.

"*Pleeease,*" I pleaded. "He really needs a home."

She looked very skeptical. It didn't seem like I

had much of a chance. Then I remembered that begging has never worked with my mom. But taking responsibility has. So I changed my tactic.

"Dad will give him shots," I said sensibly. "And I'll pay for his food and feed him every day. And I'll be in charge of changing the litter box. Plus, I can already tell that he and Frank will get along great!"

Mom looked at little Catastrophe all snuggled up in my arms, and a very faint smile began to form. "Well, all right," she finally said. "You can keep the cat."

"Yes!" I hollered, handing Catastrophe to the Fudge so I could give my mom a big hug. As I hugged my mom tight, I looked out of the corner of my eye and saw the Fudge gently rubbing his nose right up against Catastrophe's. I really couldn't believe how sweet he was being to my new cat. *Maybe he's just a blockhead around people and saves his good side for animals*, I thought.

"But that's absolutely it on the animals, Hannah," my mom warned. "There will be no gorillas, pythons, pandas..."

Pandas? Why did pandas suddenly sound so interesting?

It looked like the boys were going to win the kickball game, but I didn't really care. I had accomplished something a lot more important that day—I just very well might have saved an

Olympic career. Who knows? Maybe one day Alexis will be standing at the podium with a gold medal around her neck. Whatever happens, though, I know I will be cheering my new friend on.

Through the rest of the kickball game, I held Catastrophe in my lap. But for some reason, I couldn't stop thinking about pandas lumbering through foggy forests, chewing on bamboo.

"Where do pandas live, Catastrophe?" I asked him, staring into his green eyes. "What kinds of sounds do they make when they talk?"

Of course, he didn't answer me. Neither did my angels. But somehow I got the feeling that I'd know an awful lot about pandas very, very soon...

COOL GREEK STUFF

Acropolis—*Acro* means "high" and *polis* means "city." The Acropolis is the hill above Athens that was high up enough for ancient Greeks to be protected from their enemies. There are several very old buildings still standing there, including the Parthenon. In the spring and summer, there is an awesome sound-and-light show at night, and the whole Acropolis is flooded with bright gold lights.

Amphitheater—An outdoor theater. *Amphi* means "around," which makes sense because an amphitheater's seats wrap around the stage. Because there were no electric lights in ancient times, plays began at dawn. The audience ate breakfasts of bread, oil, and olives while they watched.

Cats—I saw plenty of stray cats in the gardens and ruins all over Athens. They're in danger, especially the little kittens, because of dogs, disease, and getting separated from their moms. An organization called Friends of the Cat (*Fili Tis Gatas* in Greek) is helping find homes for these stray cats and working to reduce the number of stray cats by asking people to neuter their own cats so baby kittens won't roam around homeless. They also educate people on how to take care of their cats.

Dance—Every area of Greece has its traditional folk dances, which have been around for centuries. The dance I tried on Captain X's ship is called *syrtaki* (soor-TOCK-ee). The music starts slow and then gets faster and faster until you're worn out, (well, atleast me). The other dance the kids were doing on the ship is called *kalamatiano* (kah-la-MAH-tee-ah-no). All the dancers follow in snake-type circles behind the leader, who waves a scarf. It's danced at many weddings and celebrations.

Language—Have you heard people say, "That's Greek to me?" They use that expression when something is unfamiliar, because the Greek alphabet looks so different from ours. A few letters are the same, like A (alpha) and B (beta). But others are really different, like G (gamma) and D (delta).

Money—*Drachmas* are Greek coins. About 300 *drachmas* equal $1.

Mythology—A collection of traditional stories with awesome superpowered characters, like the Greek gods and goddesses. A few characters you might know are: Icarus, whose wax wings melted when he flew too close to the sun, causing him to fall into the sea. *The Sirens*, sea-nymphs who hypnotized sailors with their songs, so the ships crashed against the rocks. Medusa, a winged female creature with yellow pig's teeth and snakes for hair. If you looked at her, you turned to stone. Nice, huh?

Olympic gymnastic team—In the U.S., we have a mens' and a womens' national gymnastics team. Twenty women are on the womens' team. They compete all over the world, all year round. But only six of them are chosen to compete in the Olympics. So far, there hasn't been a Greek Olympic women's gymnastics team (except, of course, the one Alexis is trying out for!).

Olympics—They began in 776 B.C. in Athens. Messengers were sent all over Greece to invite athletes and spectators to come to the event. Athletes swore an oath in front of a huge statue of Zeus, (the king of the ancient Greek gods), to play fairly and do their best. The winners were crowned with olive leaves. Nowadays, the Olympics take place every four years in different countries all over the world. And instead of olive leaves, the winners receive gold medals.

Parthenon—The most famous building on the Acropolis. It was a temple built to Athena, the Greek goddess of wisdom. It's ancient—almost 2,500 years old! It has forty-six huge columns. Lots of stray cats call it home.

Ship talk—The front of the ship is called the bow (as in "bow-wow"). The right side of the ship is called starboard, pronounced "STAR-bird." The left side is called port. Now don't ask me why—I'd just say right and left if I had my own ship. And in case anybody cares, I'd name my yacht *Seadog Frank*, after you know who.

Worry beads—A string of beads about the length of a bracelet. The beads are made of materials like jade and amber. I guess Greek people figure that when your fingers are busy fidgeting with the beads, you either have no time to worry, or you're using up all your nervous energy.

A LITTLE GREEK DICTIONARY

Adio (ah-DEE-o)—good-bye

Efharisto (eff-ha-ree-STO)—thank you

Gata (GA-ta)—cat

Komboloia (kom-bo-LOY-uh)—worry beads

Ne (nay)—yes

Oji (O-hee)—no

Parakalo (par-a-ka-LO)—please

Poli kala (po-LEE-ka-LAH)—just fine

Ti kanate? (tee-KON-uh-tay)—how are you?

Ya sou (YA-soo)—hi, bye, or cheers!

EATING GREEK-STYLE

Just like the ruins in Athens, Greek food is *very* ancient. Well, I don't mean the actual food is old, but good cooking has been handed down through the generations, and it is still great today. Did you know the word "gastronomy" is Greek? It means "the art and science of good eating."

Here's a bit of tasty trivia Captain X told me: Chef's caps—the tall white hats that restaurant chefs wear—actually came from Greece. In the 1400s, the Turks attacked Greece, so all the best Greek chefs hid in the monasteries. They dressed up like the monks, who wore tall black hats with puffy tops. Later, when the attack was over, the chefs continued to wear the hats but changed them to white so they wouldn't be confused with the monks. Now chefs all over the world wear those hats!

Here's a quick list of some of the tasty food I tried on my trip:

Anchovies—and I don't mean a thin slice, like on pizza. These are the *whole* fish, dipped in thick salt!

Baklava—a sweet pastry dessert dripping with honey and nuts. Majorly yummy!

Dolmades—a grape leaf wrapped around rice and meat.

Feta cheese—white goat cheese that's very strong and salty.

Octopus—not my favorite, but I dared myself to try it. I could see the suction cups still on the legs!

Olives—they're wrinkly and black, and cured in seawater and olive oil.

Souvlaki—what we call gyros in America. They're usually lamb wrapped in pita bread, filled with a whole bunch of stuff, like tomatoes, onions, yogurt, and sometimes even French fries!

Spanakopita—a spinach and feta-cheese pie.

Squid—they're cut in circles and fried, like onion rings, and served with lemon.

When I got home, I wanted to make a Greek dinner to celebrate the furry new addition to our family! So Grandma Zoe helped me make a Greek salad in Catastrophe's honor. It's easy—want to try?

CATASTROPHE'S GREEK SALAD

Lettuce—torn bite-sized
Tomatoes—cut in wedges
Onions—thinly sliced
Green peppers—thinly sliced
Greek olives
Cucumbers—peeled and sliced
Feta cheese—cut in little pieces
(Use more of what you like best and less of
what you don't like as much.)

1. Mix together in a big bowl.
2. Now shake oregano and pepper over
   the salad. Shake as much as you think
   you'd like.
3. Then mix up your favorite salad
   dressing and toss some onto your salad.

There you have it—
Catastrophe's Greek Salad!

Here's a sneak peek at

Hannah and the Angels #10: Panda-monium in China

We made our way into the foggy forest, quiet as deer, trying not to snap any twigs beneath our hiking boots. Mist hung from the branches like pale, mysterious veils. I felt like I'd landed in the middle of a fairy tale.

Suddenly I stopped, frozen. In the silence of the forest, I heard a whimper. It sounded like a baby. I looked at Su Lin. Her eyes were huge with wonder. The two of us stood dead still, not making a sound. In this incredibly quiet place, even breathing seemed loud.

We listened hard. We heard rustling. Then a quiet munching sound, like somebody eating cereal out of the box. Su Lin nodded toward a far tree. I slowly lifted my binoculars to my eyes and scanned up the wet tree trunk, all the way to the high misty green leaves.

I saw movement. I turned the dial of my binoculars to focus. Something furry—and way too large to be up that high—was peacefully nibbling on a green branch. I zoomed in and gasped.

A panda! And it was *huge*, more awesome than I'd imagined. It was snuggled into the tree limbs like it was lounging on a living-room couch, munching on snacks. Then it slowly somersaulted down to a lower branch, rolled onto the snowy ground, and looked my way.

**Available wherever books are sold
in October 2000!**